PUFFIN BOOKS

SALT

Maurice Gee is one of New Zealand's best-known writers for adults and children. He has won a number of literary awards, including the Wattie Award, the Deutz Medal for Fiction, the New Zealand Fiction Award, the New Zealand Children's Book of the Year Award and the Prime Minister's Award for Literary Achievement.

Maurice Gee's children's novels include *Gool, The Limping Man, The Fat Man, The Fire-Raiser, Under the Mountain* and *The O Trilogy*. Maurice lives in Nelson with his wife Margareta, and has two daughters and a son.

PUFFIN BOOKS
Published by the Penguin Group
Penguin Group (NZ), 67 Apollo Drive, Rosedale,
North Shore 0632, New Zealand (a division of Pearson New Zealand Ltd)
Penguin Group (USA) Inc., 375 Hudson Street,
New York, New York 10014, USA
Penguin Group (Canada), 90 Eglinton Avenue East, Suite 700, Toronto,
Ontario, M4P 2Y3, Canada (a division of Pearson Penguin Canada Inc.)
Penguin Books Ltd, 80 Strand, London, WC2R 0RL, England
Penguin Ireland, 25 St Stephen's Green,
Dublin 2, Ireland (a division of Penguin Books Ltd)
Penguin Group (Australia), 250 Camberwell Road, Camberwell,
Victoria 3124, Australia (a division of Pearson Australia Group Pty Ltd)
Penguin Books India Pvt Ltd, 11, Community Centre,
Panchsheel Park, New Delhi – 110 017, India
Penguin Books (South Africa) (Pty) Ltd, 24 Sturdee Avenue,
Rosebank, Johannesburg 2196, South Africa

Penguin Books Ltd, Registered Offices: 80 Strand, London, WC2R 0RL, England

First published by Puffin Books, 2007. This edition 2010

Copyright © Maurice Gee, 2007

The right of Maurice Gee to be identified as the author of this work in terms of
section 96 of the Copyright Act 1994 is hereby asserted.

Designed by Mary Egan
Typeset by Pindar NZ, Auckland, New Zealand
Map by Nick Keenleyside
Cover figures by Athena Sommerfeld
Printed and bound in Australia by Griffin Press

ISBN 978 0 14 330545 3

A catalogue record for this book is available
from the National Library of New Zealand.

www.penguin.co.nz

MIX
Paper from
responsible sources
FSC® C009448

SALT

MAURICE GEE

PUFFIN BOOKS

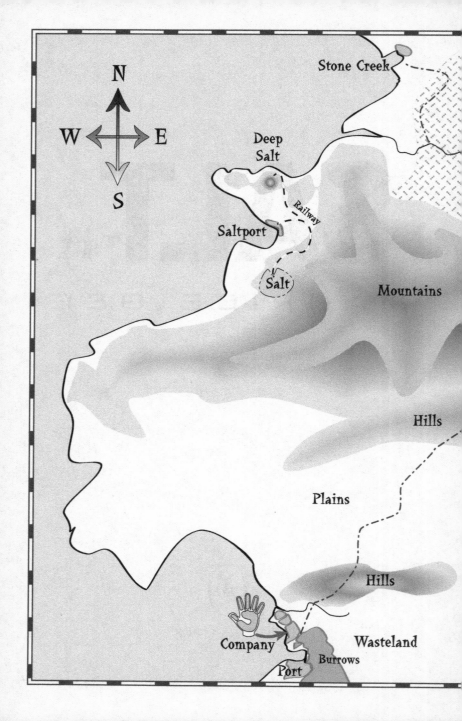

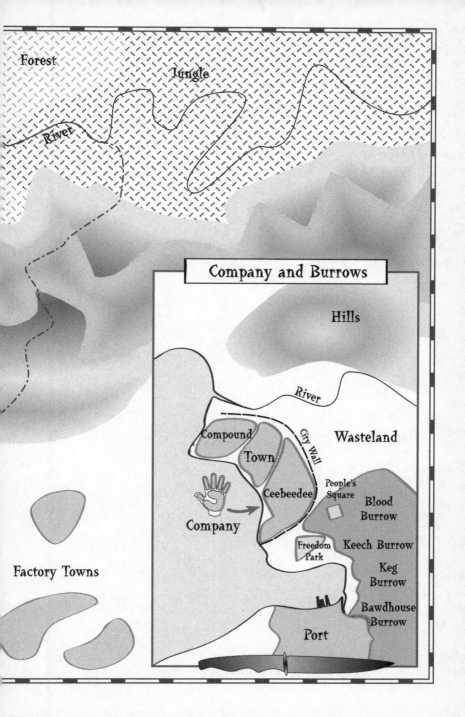

ONE

The Whips, as silent as hunting cats, surrounded Blood Burrow in the hour before sun-up and began their sweep as the morning dogs began to howl. Rain fell heavily that day, washing the streets and overflowing the gutters. The grey tunics of the Whips turned black in the downpour, their helmets shone like beetle wings, and the sparks that jumped from their fingers as they herded their recruits fizzed and spat like sewer gas.

They took ninety men, some from their hovels, some from the ruins, and prodded them, howling, to the raised southern edge of People's Square, where the paving stones had not yet slipped into the bog. Brown water lapped the buildings on the northern side. Cowl the Liberator, crying Liberty or Death, raised his marble head above the rushes. Mosquitoes bred underneath his tongue. The Whips, as custom required, paused in their herding and mouthed 'Cowl the Murderer' before going on.

A cart with a covered platform and canvas aprons at the sides and back waited on the stones. A clerk sat at a desk under the awning, with a sheaf of forms under his palm and a quill pen, curved like a blade, in his other hand. His uniform was paler than the Whips' (and dry) and had the Company symbol, an open hand, blazoned on the tunic. He frowned at the rabble herded in front of him, and drew his head back in a vain attempt to avoid the stench of rotting shirts and festering bodies.

'Sergeant.'

'Sir?'

'Is this your best effort? My orders are two hundred fit for work.'

The Whip sergeant swallowed and seemed to shrink, knowing he and his men would earn no bonus, even though they had chased hard, sparing none. 'They fled like rats. They have holes and runways everywhere.'

'And your job is to know them and bring me no starvelings, no half-dead.'

'They pretend, sir. This one –' he prodded a near-naked man, making him whimper – 'he ran like a marsh deer. Now he stoops. And this – he has swallowed dirt. It makes him vomit.'

'Enough. I know their tricks. Count.'

'Ninety, sir.'

'Silence them. And the women too.'

The Whips raised their electric hands and shot fizzing bolts into the air and the howling stopped. Outside the ring of guards, the wives and children of the ninety fell silent. Some kept their mouths wide in cries they dared not utter, while others wept soundlessly, their tears mingling with the rain, which fell more heavily, making puddles round their unclad feet.

The clerk stood up under the awning. 'Men,' he cried, widening his mouth in a smile, 'this is your great day. You are chosen to serve Company in its glorious enterprise. Daily we grow in comfort and prosperity. In this you share. Who serves Company serves mankind. Raise your voices now and give thanks.'

The men closest to the Whips made a few ragged shouts, 'Long live Company. Praise to Company,' but somewhere a woman shrieked, 'Murderers!' And from the ruined buildings round the square cries like echoes came from doorways and windows: 'Murderers, thieves!'

The clerk was untroubled. His speech was part of procedure, and the shouts and cries, and the howling and tears, were something he expected on recruiting days. He sat down and yawned behind his hand.

'Examination,' he said.

A Whip prodded a man into the space before the cart, then, with his gloves turned off, stripped off his clothing with raking sweeps of his iron hands. The man, young but stooped and thin, stood shivering in the rain.

'No need for the hose today,' said the clerk, but he yawned again while his underlings sprayed the man's body with disinfected water from a tank behind his wagon.

'Name?'

'Heck,' the man whispered.

The clerk took his quill and wrote on a form.

'Deformities?' he said to a third underling who had stepped down from the cart.

'None.'

'Sores?'

'Multiple. Feet and legs.'

'Condition?'

'E.'

The clerk ran his eyes over the man's body. 'You bring me trash,' he said to the sergeant.

'Sir, he is fast. He goes like a mud-crab. He will fit in narrow places.'

'Perhaps.' The clerk frowned at Heck. 'Saltworker,' he said.

'No,' cried the man, falling to his knees. 'Not salt. I'll go to the farms. I'll go on the ships. In the name of Company, I pray you, not salt.'

'Brand him,' said the clerk, tossing a marker to the underling.

The man beckoned his helpers for the acid bucket and the brush. He fitted the metal marker on Heck's forehead while a Whip held him still, and swiped the brush across the stencil. 'Who joins Company joins history. Your time begins,' he intoned, ignoring Heck's screaming as the acid burned.

'Name him,' said the clerk.

The underling read from the marker: 'S97406E.'

The clerk wrote.

'Is there a woman? Quickly. Come.'

A woman doubled up with age scuttled through the ring of Whips and stood in front of the cart.

'You are his?' said the clerk.

'His mother, sir. He has no wife. He could not keep a woman.'

The clerk shrugged. 'Give it to her.'

The underling handed an iron token to the crone, who seized it and hugged it to her breast.

'Show this at the Ottmar gate on the morning of the last day of each month. Company will pay you one groat. Nothing if it is lost. Do you understand?'

'Long life to Company. Company cares,' said the woman. She scuttled back through the Whips, with the marker hidden in her rags.

'Company cares,' the clerk replied, speaking by rote. 'Next.'

The rain continued to fall. The numbering and branding went on until mid-morning. Under the cart, Hari knelt on the stones, shifting only to ease his legs and holding his knife ready to stab. The horses knew he was there but he had made a bond with them as he found his hiding place. Now and then he slipped his hand under the canvas apron and touched each one on the fetlock, as light as a fly, renewing that bond. He had cut a flap like an eyelid in the side-canvas, and he watched as each recruit was held and branded and each wife or daughter given a token, and he was filled with hatred and rage, which he had to hold down, and aim away at the Whips and the clerk, so it would not alarm the horses. He must keep them calm, and use them when the time was right. He watched his father, who had two names, Tarl and Knife.

He had thought they would never take his father, and Tarl himself had made a vow that he would die before letting Company enslave him. Yet here he was, held within the ring, burned on his chest and arms by electric fingers, and waiting his turn for the brand.

The early howling of the dogs had woken them that morning, in their corner of the ruined hall known as Dorm, and Hari had read the message in their howls, and run among the sleeping tribe, waking them with kicks and cries: 'The Whips are coming.'

'Wake the burrow, I'll do the streets,' his father had shouted, so Hari plunged through stairwells and runways and pits, on sloping beams, on slides of rubble, shouting his warning: 'The Whips, the Whips!' Men scurried into the dark, deeper into holes inside Blood Burrow. A hundred or more made their escape.

Tarl had chosen the more dangerous way, warning men in the shelters opening off the streets – and somehow the Whips had cornered him and locked him in their fizzing ring. Hari, at the end of his run, watching from a crevice in the base of a shattered wall by People's Square, had seen the ninety herded round the edge of the swamp, and seen with disbelief his father among them. The clerk's cart had rumbled by, a body length from his nose, heading for its place by the south wall. Hari had not thought; he had acted, the way the feral dogs, the way the deep-crawling, invisible rats had taught him. He darted across the stones, slid under the canvas apron, rolled between the iron-clad wheels and fastened himself like a cockroach to the underside of the cart. He felt the horses sense him and replied in a silent whisper: Brother horse, sister horse, I am here, I am you.

Eighty-nine men were stripped and branded and named and stood shivering in the bitter rain, each with his hands tied at his back and a rope halter fastening him to the man in front. His father was the last, and Hari, watching through his eyehole in the canvas, saw why he had worked himself into that position. Inside Tarl's ragged shirt, in its ratskin sheath, his knife was hidden. He had won space for his throwing arm. The clerk would die. Hari heard his father's intention like a whisper.

No, he tried to whisper back, I have a better way. He was too late.

Tarl writhed and cowered, with his limbs locked in crooked shapes as though by disease. The Whip stepped close, turning off his gloves. He raised his iron fingers to strip Tarl's clothes, and in that moment Tarl became himself – stepped in and out, with his black-bladed knife in his hand, and slashed like the blow of a fangcat. The Whip fell back, shrieking, as his cheek between his helmet's eye- and jaw-piece opened up.

A single leap sideways gave Tarl room. He turned in the air and landed facing the clerk. The knife spun in his hand as he reversed it. But even as it sped away with a whipping sound Hari saw his father's error. The blade was slippery with blood, and Tarl's fingers had slid at the last moment, lowering the trajectory. The knife struck the edge of the desk. It bounded back and fell on the stones. And already Whips, with gloves sparking at lethal power, surrounded his father and moved in.

'Hold him. Don't kill him,' cried the clerk.

They paused an arm's length away and held Tarl immobile in their hissing ring. His clothes began to steam and smoulder, and the clerk cried, 'Back. Further back. I want to see him.'

The Whips retreated a single step.

'Strip him,' said the clerk.

The Whip sergeant raked Tarl's body, making him scream. Tarl stood naked in the rain.

'Yes, I see. No crooked man after all. You will serve Company well. What a pity it is we cannot use your knife skills. I might have posted you to Company Guard. But after attacking a Whip and trying to assassinate me, you have lost your chance.'

'I will join no Company. I belong to myself. I'm a free man,' Tarl cried.

The clerk gave a smile and said patiently, 'Yes, that is true. Everyone is free. But freedom means serving Company. Is that not understood in the burrows?'

'You use us to enrich yourselves. You starve us and turn us into slaves.'

'There is a time of hardship,' said the clerk. 'For everyone. But Company works for all and the benefit will reach here soon. It comes down like the soft rain, even into Blood Burrow, you will see. Perhaps it is time we sent educators here. But enough talk. What is your name?'

'I have none for Company. It is mine,' said Tarl.

'Then keep it,' said the clerk. 'I'll make you a new one.' He spoke to his assistant, who punched out a stencil. The clerk threw it down to the underling.

'Brand him,' he said.

Two Whips with gloves at quarter power forced Tarl to his knees. Even so, his limbs jerked with pain. The underlings, one with the stencil, one with the acid, branded him. Tarl cried out, but not with the burning. 'I do not accept this. I am Tarl.'

The clerk picked up his quill. 'Not any more, I'm afraid. Yes, man, read it.'

The underling obeyed, and a moan of fear went up from the haltered prisoners and the women gathered by the swamp.

'DS936A,' the man read.

Under the cart Hari closed his eyes in terror. DS was Deep Salt, the furthest reaches of the deepest tunnels of the mine. Men sent there never returned to the surface. What they dug for nobody knew, and after a time, one by one, they vanished. No bodies, no traces of a body, were ever found. It was said the salt worms took them, or salt tigers, or salt rats, but these were make-believe creatures no one had seen. It was said their souls were sucked down into the dark lake at the centre of the world and locked in cages forever. Hari believed it. He knelt with his forehead on the stones, shaking with fear. The cart horses whinnied and rippled their hides as though stung by flies.

Outside, the Whips stepped back from Tarl, and after a moment he rose from his knees.

'I am still, I am always, a free man,' he said, but his voice was thin and afraid.

'Who you are is DS936A,' said the clerk. 'And I offer my congratulations. It is the first time I have given an A. Your woman will get two groats instead of one. Where is she?'

'I have no woman. And I will take nothing from Company.'

'Then Company is spared the expense, which is to the good. Bind him, and make it tight.'

The Whips obeyed, while Hari, under the cart, raised himself from the stones and crept to his eyehole again. Stay, he commanded the horses, do not move. He saw how the Whips pulled his father's halter tight and tied double knots to bind his hands. But Tarl had no man fastened behind him. A single knife-slash would cut him free.

'Let no man think he can change his destiny, which is service to Company,' said the clerk. 'You will march now, ninety servants in the glorious enterprise, to the dispersal centre, where you will find clean tunics, each emblazoned with the open hand, and food, good food, enough to satisfy strong men like you. Company cares.'

'Company cares,' murmured several of the recruits, for 'food' and 'enough' were words seldom heard in the burrows.

The clerk smiled. 'From there you will go to your new work – to Ships, to Coal, to Farm, to Factory, to Granary, to Salt –' he smiled again – 'and to Deep Salt. Each will serve out his time, and payment will be made to your women here at home. Company cares. And when you have made your contribution and wish to labour no more, you will retire to a Golden Village as honoured workers of Company, and your women will join you to live out your lives in quiet enjoyment. That is the happy future Company prescribes for you! Now march like men. March like servants in our enterprise.'

'And march to your deaths,' Tarl cried, 'for there is no retirement. You will work until you die. That is the only use Company has for you.'

The Whip sergeant stepped at him with his hands raised, but the clerk cried, 'Leave him. Let him rant. He goes to Deep Salt, and it is true, no man returns from there. But let me ask

15

you, fellow –' he squinted at Tarl's forehead – 'DS936A. Are there any more hidden in the burrows like you? Do you have followers, do you spread your poison among our happy citizens there? We must investigate. A brother perhaps? A son to follow in your ways?'

'No,' Tarl said, 'no son.' But he spoke too quickly, for the clerk said, 'Ah. I must make a note,' and turned to pick up his quill.

Under the cart, Hari waited another moment. Whips stood too close to his father. But he must act, there might not be another chance. He sent a questing thread out from his mind to the horses, found them, and whispered silently: Brother horse, sister horse, the black fly stings your rump.

The two beasts lurched forward, rearing and whinnying. The cart bucked and leaned, and the clerk's desk skidded sideways, carrying him with it. It balanced on the edge of the tray, then tipped off. He thrust out his arm to save himself and one of the iron cart-wheels crushed his elbow on the stones. His shriek rose like a sharp spear into the sky.

Hari slid back as the cart advanced. The canvas flap at the rear brushed over him and he sprang to his feet in the open. The acid bucket stood close, and he seized it and flung it one-handed at the two underlings. They danced, screaming, as the acid burned. Hari sprang sideways, quick as a cat. He stabbed with his knife into a helmet joint of the nearest Whip as the man fumbled with his glove, but the joint shut as the Whip fell, holding the blade as though in a vise and ripping the knife from Hari's hand.

'My knife, Hari,' Tarl screamed.

Hari saw it lying by the wheel of the cart and scooped it up, but his advantage of surprise was gone. The Whips who had run to help the clerk abandoned him and rushed back to surround Tarl, while others who had been posted at the gates of People's Square came running around the side of the swamp. Hari sprang sideways. He felt the heat of a Whip hand strike in the space he had left; heard the deputy clerk, standing on the cart, cry, 'Take him alive.' He dived low, skidding on his belly across the stones, passed between Whips' feet and came upright beside his father. He slashed with the black-bladed knife, and the rope linking Tarl to the man in front parted like a cotton thread. There was no time to cut Tarl's hands free, for the Whips were closing in, with yellow bolts jumping from their fingertips.

Again Hari flung his thought-spear at the horses: The black fly stings. The black fly bites. The animals whinnied with pain and plunged against their traces, jumping the cart forward. The linked water cart tumbled on its side, pinning three Whips on the stones. Hari and his father sprang through the gap, but the Whip sergeant, sprawling on the ground, lunged as they went by and clamped Tarl's heel in his burning hand. Tarl fell, screaming, and Hari, two steps ahead, felt the pain too, so close was their bond. He fell on his knees, crying out, and would have turned to help his father, but Tarl, in the grip of the iron hand, mouthed: 'Go.'

Whips were only a body length away. Hari felt their heat. He turned and plunged into the crowd of women.

'A purse for whoever takes the boy,' cried the deputy clerk.

Some of the women clawed at him; others parted, making way, then closed again. But the Whips, close behind, with burning hands, knocked them aside like stalks of corn. Hari had no time to pause at the edge of the swamp. He plunged through the rushes, mud sucking at his feet, then flung himself into the brown water where it deepened, and clawed his way down with his father's knife clutched in his fist. Deep, deeper, he went, blind in the murk, out of reach of the iron men. Swimming was unknown in the burrows, where no water flowed except in drains, and the scummy ponds and yellow swamps that lay in deep basements and abandoned squares and parks were believed to be poisonous; but Hari, taught by the old Survivor, Lo, had learned how to worm his way into the minds of the giant rats that lived deeper in the ruins than men could go, and had found the place where their swimming instinct had its home, and had learned the skill. The ponds, the swamps, were part of his highway through the burrows. He swam with his belly sliding on mud, probing with his father's knife, until he felt it strike the sunken pedestal of Cowl the Liberator's statue. With his breath almost gone, he circled to the back, then climbed the Liberator as if he were a tree and broke the surface of the pond beside Cowl's giant head. He put one foot in his wide mouth, hauled himself up on a shaggy eyebrow and lay on the slope of Cowl's forehead, catching his breath.

Most of the Whips had given him up for dead, but the sergeant still watched. 'There, the boy,' he cried. 'He swims like a rat.'

The clerk was on his feet, with his crushed arm dripping blood. 'Kill him,' he shrieked. 'Use your bolt guns. I authorise it.'

The Whips drew their weapons from their belts and flicked them on. Hari, watching from his perch, knew he had a moment while the charge built up. He saw his father climb painfully to his feet, his leg half-dead still from the sergeant's glove.

'Tarl,' Hari cried, 'I'll come for you.'

'Stay here. Your job's here,' Tarl answered. The nearest Whip felled him with a sideways blow.

'Kill the boy,' whimpered the clerk. Then he fainted on the stones.

The bolt guns were charged. They were clumsy weapons that could not be aimed accurately, but the bolt of energy they threw would blast a hole in a stone wall. Hari waited until the sergeant levelled his weapon. Then he scrambled across the top of Cowl's head and slid onto his submerged shoulder.

'Company dies,' he shouted, and flung himself into the water as the sergeant's bolt fell in its arc towards him.

This time he stayed shallow, for it was a longer swim. He held his father's knife in his teeth and went like a mud-frog, arms and legs stroking in unison. The pool was deepest where it met the wall of a ruined building on the north side of the square between two gates. He meant to come up there, and would have time for only a single breath before the bolt guns were fired again.

Then I must make them think I'm drowned, he thought, but Tarl will know.

His hands touched the wall. He fixed his feet on jutting stones and propelled himself up. Beyond Cowl's broken head the sergeant was watching, and other Whips, their bolt guns raised, were waiting by the gates at the edge of the pond. Tarl struggled to his feet again. He made an agonised shout: 'Never let them take you.'

Hari had no breath to reply. He took the knife, his father's knife, from his teeth and raised it above his head, knowing Tarl would understand. Bolts hissed towards him. He sank again, and was punched by detonations, burned by water that boiled as they struck, but he had marked his place and knew his way. Down again, and sideways, counting the handholds in the wall, until, four body lengths under the surface, he found the hole he was seeking, blown in the base of the wall by cannon bolts in Company's Freedom War. The masonry was thick and the hole narrowed to his shoulders' width on the inner side. He wriggled through, fighting slimy weed that hung like curtains, bent his body upwards, inside the wall, and slithered along tunnels in the drowned masonry, praying that no new fall of stone had closed the passage, and that he would not meet a king rat here.

At last he broke into the air and freed his knife from his teeth and lay across a shattered door, gasping for breath. Then he hauled himself up through tangles of broken beam and plank until he reached the light. It pierced in rays through the building's roof. He was in a vast room, for banquets and dancing in the old days, he supposed – although he had no idea what banquets and dancing were. Everything had been scavenged generations ago. Rubble and rotting timbers lay on the inlaid floor. Hari did not pause, although in the past he had spent hours in the room, shifting rubble and scraping the floor clean so that he might wonder at the coloured scenes of trees and animals and people inlaid in green and red and yellow tiles.

There were no windows, no openings to People's Square. Hari ran through halls and passages, crawled in tunnels of broken stone, climbed through floors and ceilings, and slid through walls where charred timber stood like blackened teeth. He crept on his knees around a hole opening in the floor of the watchtower over East Gate. Below him, a Whip kept guard, with his bolt gun holstered and his gloves humming at low power. Hari went by, as soundless as a cat. Then he ran again and came at last to a building on the south side of the square. A window opened in the wall above the clerk's cart. It was blocked with timber except for a small hole at the bottom where the frame had been forced out like a fractured bone. Hari inched forward and the square came into view.

The rain had stopped and the sun was shining. Half a dozen haltered men with their hands set free were tipping the water cart back on its wheels. Tarl was not among them. He was chained to an iron ring on the clerk's cart, and the Whip sergeant was guarding him.

Hari sent his thought thread to the horses: Brother horse, sister horse, I'm sorry I caused you pain. I ask you, travel slowly so my father doesn't fall.

He did not know in what form the silent messages Lo had taught him to send reached animals, but the horses pricked their ears up as though they heard.

I thank you, Hari said, and turned his eyes back to his father. They would take him across the desert to the mines, and down the shafts into Deep Salt, where no worker ever came out. Hari held the black-bladed knife in front of his eyes. 'Don't die,' he whispered. 'I'll save you.' It was a foolhardy promise and one there was no way to keep, but it hardened in him, swelled in him, beat like his heart in his chest, and he knew he would try.

Below him the women and children drifted away. The acid-burned underlings bound the clerk's broken elbow to his side. He had woken from his faint and groaned with pain. The deputy clerk strutted importantly, ordering Whips to singe the men raising the water cart. The Whips pinned under it were carried away. One was dead.

The underlings lifted the clerk onto his cart and laid him down. Hari, seeing how close Tarl stood, thought: My father could kill him now with a single bite. He could tear his throat out like a hunting cat. But Tarl only smiled and said to the clerk, 'You hurt now but soon you'll hurt more. You're a broken part. Company will throw you away.'

'It's not true,' screeched the clerk. 'Company cares.'

'Your quota was two hundred men and you bring ninety. And you bring a dead Whip. Company doesn't like mistakes. Perhaps you'll join me in Deep Salt.'

'Kill this man. Kill him,' cried the clerk.

But the sergeant made no move and the deputy clerk said, 'We must not waste an able-bodied man. He belongs to Company.'

'You see,' Tarl said. 'Already someone stands in your place.'

'You will die in Deep Salt,' hissed the clerk. 'Salt worms will eat you. Your soul will be sucked down into the dark.'

'So be it,' Tarl said, shrugging.

'And your son is dead. He drowned like a rat. Think of that.'

'He did not die a slave, he died free,' Tarl said. 'He has conquered Company today.'

He knows I'm not dead, Hari thought. He knows I'm close and can hear. He tried to send a message to his father: I'll come to Deep Salt and set you free. Tarl had never been able to hear in that way. But he feels me, Hari thought. He knows I'm here.

He watched as the carts rolled round the sloping stones by the swamp, until the Whips and clerks and underlings were at the gate. Tarl turned his head at the last moment and looked past Cowl's sunken head. His eyes found the hole in the broken window frame.

He knows, Hari thought, and he risked pushing out his fist that clenched the black knife.

His father nodded once, and was gone.

I'll save you, Hari thought.

He drew back his hand, and made his way down corridors and runways into the burrows.

TWO

It was true that Tarl had no woman. She had died in the sickness of 77, leaving Hari without a mother. He was three years old. The sickness had nearly taken him too. He wore the scars on his face.

His father raised him, carrying him on his back or on his shoulders until the boy was able to run at his side. Hari learned every slide and hole and tunnel in Blood Burrow, perched on Tarl's shoulders or climbing after him on broken walls or deep in the ruins towards Port. They scavenged in the streets around the closed citadel, Ceebeedee, where Company conducted its business, and along the fortified wall enclosing the corridor to the sea. Above the bay, on a green hill called Compound, the owners and shareholding families had their mansions. When he was older, Hari came to know every inch of the wall, even though, to learn the far side, he had to circle round through the empty lands at the back of the suburbs beyond Ceebeedee. He was afraid of that journey, for there were few places to hide from the young men from the Families who rode out from the walls to hunt burrows scavengers for sport, or from feral dogs roaming in packs. Yet he took the risk, for the sight of the mansions in Compound and the flowering trees and the carriages rolling in the streets, and creatures he scarcely recognised as human, their bodies were so tall and fat and white. Their skirts and cloaks were made of cloth that shimmered in colours only seen in the burrows in bits of broken glass and scraps of tile.

He climbed against the downflow of drains into Compound. He slid under grilles in the night, submerged, and came up on the hill behind the crescent of mansions facing the sea. Roads as broad as city blocks ran through the parks surrounding them. Hari sped across like a hunting cat into the gardens and slid, like a rat now, into the lily ponds. Sometimes, in the warm months, he would lie in a pond all night, moving only to drink the water trickling from fountains or creep to the mansion windows and hide in the flowering trees, wrapped close to the trunk. He watched the people inside – he knew they were people, like him; Lo had told him – watched them sipping drinks from tiny glasses and eating food from huge plates laid before them by serving men who must have had their tongues cut out for they never spoke. Before dawn broke he crept around to the back of the mansions and hunted in the rubbish bins for scraps of food (no feral dogs here, no dogs at all, and no cats, for Compound families had no fondness for animals). Carrying bones to gnaw on, he scouted along the cliffs, working out ways of escape, places where he might climb or jump, if guards ever saw him. He circled the giant marble hand raised on the cliff edge as a memorial to Families slain in Cowl's revolution. Then he followed the drains down to the sea, where he slept in caves in the cliffs while day lasted, before the dangerous journey back to Blood Burrow in the night.

Tarl knew about these expeditions and encouraged them, trusting Hari not to be caught. He questioned the boy closely

24

about everything he had seen – numbers of guards, location of barracks, weak places in the wall, drains that surfaced in unpatrolled places – preparing for the rebellion Hari knew would never come. There was no way the starved population of the burrows could ever be organised to fight, and nothing to fight with; and, for most of them, nothing to fight for except food. There had to be some new thing – a new idea, a new ally, a new source of strength. Lo, the old Survivor, had taught the boy this. Hari was the only person in the burrows who knew that Lo still had a voice and could speak.

Hari ran and scrambled for an hour after leaving the window above People's Square, going deeper all the time, past the dangerous edges of Keech Burrow and Keg Burrow, cutting through Bawdhouse Burrow, where women screeched invitations to him, heading for the forbidden district of Port, where Whips patrolled the streets and Company vessels lined the wharves two deep. (Hari had seen the ships on nights when he crept and swam through the piles under the wharves.) Lo's cell was in an abandoned tongue of Bawdhouse poking into Port. On stormy nights the old Survivor could hear the sound of the sea. He came from a family of ocean-farers and had sailed as a mess boy before a cannon flash blinded him in the war Company called Liberation War in the year it called Year One. He was ninety-nine years old, the last survivor of the war left in the burrows.

Hari stopped by the curtain blocking the narrow entry to Lo's tiny room. He waited, panting softly from his run, and soon Lo's voice, creaking like an old door, said, 'I hear you, boy. Come in. There's no need to wait.'

Hari pulled the curtain aside, stepped in and let it fall. The room was dark but he knew where Lo lay on his bed of rags in the corner.

'I bring no food or water. I'm sorry,' he said.

'I have enough. And I need little. You've been running, boy.'

'Company has taken my father.'

Lo was silent. Hari heard him shifting, heard him groan as he struggled to sit up. He stepped forward, using the sounds as a guide, and took the old man's shoulders – bones as thin as rat bones – and helped him find a comfortable place against the wall.

'Thank you, boy. You can let in light if it will help.'

Hari found the wedge of stone blocking a hole in the wall and pulled it out. The light made scarcely any difference, but after a moment he was able to see Lo dimly – a man shrunken with age and with years of near-starvation, sitting on his bed-rags in the dust, with only a scrap of cloth about his loins. Hari wondered what kept him alive.

'I don't know,' Lo answered, hearing the thought. 'I will not see Company's end. Or even the beginnings of its end. But the beginning of beginnings, perhaps.'

'My father is gone.'

'And you grieve. That is right. None come back. You must live by your own wits now.'

'You haven't asked where they've taken him.'

'There's no need. Tarl was a free man. He was unbroken. They will take him to Deep Salt.'

Again Hari felt his innards churn at the name. His throat tightened so he could scarcely speak.

'What's in Deep Salt? Tell me,' he managed to say.

'I've heard all sorts of tales, and none of them true. Don't be afraid, boy. Salt worms, salt tigers – they're creatures that live only in men's minds. Salt rats? Perhaps. Rats are everywhere. But know this, Hari: something is there. I've heard of men sucked away in the night, sucked from the

26

places where they sleep, and they are never seen again. Those are tales too – but I have heard a whisper among the rats that such things happen. And what a rat knows . . .' He left it unfinished, but after a moment said, 'Tarl will be one who is sucked away. Others die at their labour and their fellow workers leave their bodies in the empty tunnels, where they lie forever. But the thing, whatever it is, will take Tarl.'

'How do you know?' Hari cried.

'I've told you, boy, between what happens now and what will happen a curtain hangs, as black as my world has been since the cannon flash, but now and then a hand takes mine and leads me to the edge of tomorrow, and lifts the curtain aside, and I see . . .'

'What do you see? Do you see my father? Do you see him now?'

'Only shadows, Hari. But he seems to stand up from where he has fallen, and there's a voice that whispers: "Follow me." I can't tell if it's a friendly thing or something evil – but he stands . . .'

'And follows? He follows the voice?'

'So it seems to me. But the curtain closes, Hari, and the night that I live in comes back.'

'I came to tell you . . .'

'Yes, what?'

'That I've promised to save him.'

'Ah,' Lo said. He was silent for a long time. Then Hari saw his mouth widen in a grimace. 'Yes,' he said, 'that is what you must do.'

'Do you see something? Is the curtain lifting?'

'No, boy. Nothing comes. But I think you must do what you must do. Follow your voice when it calls.' He grimaced again. 'I'll be sorry to lose you. I'll die when you're gone . . .'

'No.'

'You've kept me alive. Teaching you has been a reason to put my face to the hole in the wall and feel the breeze and hear the sea breaking. Hari, you alone know the things I've known. The men who told me the tales and the history, and the men, the women too, who learned how to reach into the minds of the animals, and taught me the skill, are dead long ago, and you are left. I found no others.'

'My father. I've told him.'

'And did he know? Did he learn?'

'He learned enough to fight Company. And teach me how to fight.'

'And that is all?'

'He could not . . . it was too hard for him, reaching inside the rat or cat. And the stories you told me and I told him, they made him angry and he would sharpen his knife on a stone and hunt in the burrows for a king rat, and cry as he killed: "Company dies!"' Hari felt tears on his cheeks. 'That is all.'

'But you know there must be other ways.'

'Yes.'

'And I've told you how things came to be.'

'Yes.'

'Tell me, before you go.'

Hari swallowed. He did not want to go over the story again: the invasion, the defeats, the years of slavery. He wanted Lo to tell him how to find Deep Salt and free his father. But he knew the old man never asked for anything without a reason, so he wet his lips and began: 'There were centuries, long centuries, before Company came. Life was good. Our city was Belong and our name The Belongers. Our ships went out from Freeport, far into the west and north, to harvest the seas. Our lands stretched south and west, grain fields and farms, as far as men had ever travelled

– to the jungles and the deserts that lie beyond. Men came from distant countries, came with their caravans and ships, to trade with us, bringing goods we needed and taking goods away. And we, the Belongers, were happy. And then one day a black ship came. We had not known there were lands beyond the lands we knew. A black ship with white sails and a red open hand marked on the flag. Its name was *Open Hand* and it came from a place called Company.'

Hari felt his tongue grow thick and refuse to talk. That day when the black ship – bigger than any that had ever been seen before – sailed into Freeport was the day slavery began, although all was calm at first, and friendly at first, open handed, and years went by and trade went on and many ships came from Company. But somehow those who had been young when the first ship, *Open Hand*, arrived found that as old men and women they were citizens of Belong no longer but had become servants of Company.

'They took small steps and we were greedy. They brought so many good things. Our city grew. Company set up warehouses and granaries and factories and our rulers said it was good, it brought more wealth. And then Company must have barracks too, for its soldiers, who were needed to protect its property – and we allowed it. They became our army and police. And soon our ships were not allowed to sail, they must be Company ships. Our farms were Company farms. And managers and clerks from Company ran everything. Our whole city. Our government. Everything. Their families settled our lands, and the ones who grew rich built mansions on the cliffs and put up walls and called it Compound, and we, the Belongers, were the servants there, and workers in their factories and on their ships and farms. So it went on, until we must sell ourselves to them and be slaves. Ourselves were all we had to sell. So we belonged to Company.'

'Yes, boy,' Lo said, 'you know the tale. Don't wipe your eyes. It's no shame to cry.'

Hari's tears had been silent. Had the old man known he wept because he too was weeping quietly from his blind eyes? He sat down beside Lo and went on with the story:

'Then one day in the city a Company dray with goods from the port ran over a woman selling trinkets and crushed her beneath its wheels, and the driver would not stop. He cried that he was late with his delivery and would be whipped if he delayed, and anyway the woman had not moved quickly enough, people must make way for Company, and the guard who rode with him uncurled his whip and struck the woman's children out of the way – and that was the moment the great rebellion started. Cowl the Liberator killed the guard with his knife.'

'Yes, boy, I saw it. Cowl was an honest sailor, a friend of my father, and I was riding on my father's back. Cowl jumped on the dray and killed the guard, and the driver fled. Then Cowl discovered he had a voice and he called on the people to rise against Company and take back our land, and our sea, for ourselves. Tell the tale . . .'

'It was like a tide. A great tide rising everywhere, and everyone heard the voice, in the city, on the ships, and soon in the countryside. Every man and woman found a weapon, a knife, a sickle. Every child. By nightfall Belong was free again and all the Company guards, and the managers and clerks, were dead. We stormed the ships in the port and hung the captains from the masts. We hunted Company families in Compound, in their mansions, and dragged those we captured to the cliffs and threw them off. We were fierce and cruel. Not one was left . . .'

Hari swelled with fierceness himself, and stabbed and slashed the air with his knife – his father's knife. But, as always when he told the tale, or remembered it, his savagery leaked away and he shrank small.

Lo's voice, sad and creaking, asked, 'What happened after that?'

'Looting, destruction, chaos, death. Ten leaders in the city, each with his army. Brigands in the countryside, murdering and burning. Men who were kings for a week or a day. Until Cowl the sailor burst from Port and cleaned out the city with his men and drove all the little kings away. Then he made a government and tried to put Belong back together, and slowly it began to be as it had been before Company came. The farms began to raise their cattle and plant their crops. It began, we began . . .'

'And then?'

Hari swallowed. 'Cowl made himself king.'

Lo uttered a groan of despair. His head sank on his breast as though he could not hold it upright any more.

'I don't need to go on,' Hari said.

'Tell it. All parts must be told.'

Hari wet his lips. 'He made himself king. He declared that he must rule alone, that parliament would weaken the state. He put up statues of himself. Cowl the Liberator became Cowl the King. He made a court, with courtiers who lived in the mansions. He built an army and planned the conquest of other lands. And soon we found that we were slaves again. And all the while, in their home beyond the lands we knew, Company was getting ready to come back. Company was stronger, far stronger than we knew.'

'I was ten years old when they came,' Lo said. 'I was back from my first voyage as cabin boy on my father's ship. We lay in port on a fine morning and saw a cloud rise out of the sea, and swell, and grow. It was the black fleet, a hundred ships, boy, great iron ships with engines that roared, and the red

31

hand painted on their sides. Engines driven by steam. We had never seen steam used in that way. Guns that threw bolts of fire, and we had crossbows and spears . . .'

'Company,' Hari sobbed.

'Company returned.'

'And they stood off Freeport for ten days and nights, firing their cannons into the town until there was no building left whole, until Cowl had no army left. Then Company sent its troops ashore and the slaughter began, and only people who fled into the country survived, or those who hid deep in the ruins. They captured Cowl and his generals and threw them off the cliff, the way we had thrown their families. They marched into the countryside and conquered all the towns; they marched as far as the jungles and the desert, taking everything. And here in Belong they let the ruins lie, as a reminder to those who survived, but built Ceebeedee and a new Compound and Port – and they ruled, while we lived in the ruins. In the burrows. We lived like rats. I will . . . I will . . .'

'Yes, boy, what will you do?'

'I'll drive them out. I'll kill them.'

'As your father would have done?'

'Yes, like my father.'

'Who was captured by the Whips and taken to Deep Salt. Hari, let me tell you, Company will not be defeated by swords and spears. Or by bolt guns either. Company will rule until the end of time.'

'No,' Hari cried.

'Unless . . .'

'Unless?'

'. . . you find another way.'

'What way?'

'I don't know. But sometimes I see the curtain of the

future twitch, and seem to see light on the other side and hear a fading whisper that might be a name. I can't be sure. And I can never raise myself and go there . . .'

'What name?'

'I don't know.'

'Is it mine? Will I fight Company? Will we be free?'

'I don't hear armies fighting. I hear a voice that whispers: "Find the way."'

'How?'

'I ask that question but no answer ever comes.'

'By saving my father?'

'If that is what you have promised. Save him if you can. And if you die there . . .' Lo shook his head. 'Hari, there's nothing we can be sure of. And perhaps I heard what I wished to hear. But now you must keep your mind on things to do. How to leave the burrows. How to travel in the mountains and the jungle. I know nothing of these matters. You must find out for yourself.'

'Where is Salt? Where is Deep Salt?'

'North. There were salt mines in the mountains when I was a boy. Perhaps they are still there.'

'How will they take my father?'

'By ship. You must go by land.'

'How?'

'By doing each day what you must do. I can tell you no more than that.'

They sat side by side, in silence, for a long time. I will leave Blood Burrow and find my father, Hari thought. It would be like stepping into the dark and not knowing where his foot might fall. He had no faith that he would hear a voice calling his name, or see a curtain lifting and a light shining ahead. That was for Lo, who had not shifted from his tiny cell for many years. It is the end for this old man, he thought.

He rose to his feet. 'I'll bring you food and water before I leave.'

'No, Hari. I have a crust of bread and a pannikin. After that, I need no more.'

'You will die?'

'Yes, I'll die. But help me feel the wind and hear the sea before you go. And say goodbye in the way I've taught you, so I can hear your true voice.'

Hari lifted Lo to his feet, put an arm around him and helped him to the hole in the wall. The old man leaned there, feeling a breeze that rose from Port and found its way through the ruins to his face. He smiled. 'The wind is rising. I can hear waves breaking far away. Leave me here, Hari. I won't shift again.'

Hari fetched his pannikin of water and crust of bread and put them on the ground where the old man would find them when he sank down. He touched his shoulder and stepped back. Then he spoke, not with his tongue but silently: Thank you, Father Lo, for all you have taught me.

For a moment no answer came. Then he felt a breeze and heard waves breaking softly in his head, and Lo's young voice, not creaking now or halting, spoke in the cavern behind his eyes: Hari, you have been the son I never had. Don't forget what I've taught you. And learn new things I haven't known.

I'll try, Hari said.

Then go where you must go. Remember me.

Hari touched Lo's arm. Then he turned and left the old man's cell and made his way back through the ruins to Blood Burrow.

He did not go to Dorm. He and his father had been outsiders in the tribe, tolerated for their fighting skills. It would be known by now that Tarl had been taken, and believed that

Hari was drowned. So let me be dead, Hari thought. It was safer that no whisper of him existed anywhere. He went instead to the wasteland that had been Freedom Park, where the largest of the packs of wild dogs came each night to sleep. They were not his friends, but not enemies either. If they caught him unprepared they would tear him to pieces for food. But if he stood in some place they could not climb to, on some jag of masonry, with his line of retreat clear in his mind, they would talk and listen in their way.

He found a gaping wall with a tumble of bricks and rotting timber below it, and climbed down silently until he crouched at head height above the resting pack. They scented him, rose clamouring – sixty dogs and bitches, some with pups at heel. Hari waited as they rushed and leaped hungrily. They had not taken many rats today. He waited until they had learned he was out of reach. Then he locked eyes with the pack leader, a brown and yellow dog, once heavy in his body but skinny now, and grey haired about his muzzle. His time as leader was nearly done.

Food, Hari spoke silently.

The dog gave a yelp of hunger.

But you must wait, Hari said, and do what I say.

One of the bitches understood and howled with despair.

There's an old man dying, Hari said. Rats will smell him out before he's dead. You must kill the rats. There will be many. Then you will eat.

It was the last thing he could do for Lo, whose mind would be too weak to repel rats as he died.

Where? said the dog.

You must let the old man die in his own time.

Then he is food? said the dog.

He is food. Leave him clean.

Crack his bones?

35

Hari knew he could not prevent it. They would get little enough meat from Lo.

Crack his bones.

Where is he?

Wait.

This was the hard part. He cast his mind about the pack, hunting for one he might speak with secretly. At the rear, behind the half-grown pups, a starved black and yellow dog limped back and forth, wanting to join in but ready to run if the leader turned on him. He had been strong once, square in his body and wide in his head, but injury had slowed him and starvation weakened him. One day the others would kill him for food.

Hari narrowed his concentration, sent a spear of thought out: Stay, dog, when they go. I will give you food.

The animal gave a yelp of surprise.

Hari turned back to the leader: Say you will wait until the old man dies.

We will wait if there are rats enough.

Hari would have to take that chance for Lo. Already it might be too late.

Then here is the way.

He pictured the route: the tunnels, broken rooms, hollow streets, falls of shattered masonry, the tongue of ruined city poking into Port, and lastly the curtain hiding the entrance to Lo's cell.

Run silently or the rats will hear, he said.

Do not try to teach dogs how to hunt.

The leader gave a bark, turned once, and set off in a hungry lope across the wasted park. In a moment the pack was gone. Only the black and yellow dog remained.

Food, it whined.

Soon, Hari said. Follow me. And obey.

He jumped down from his perch and ran across the park, in the opposite direction from the pack. The dog followed, limping. Hari skirted Dorm. He climbed towards the walls of Ceebeedee. Twice he lifted the dog up barriers of stone too high for him. Then he wriggled along sinuous paths and crawled through tunnels and came to an iron door set in an undamaged wall. The dog stood at his heels, whining piteously. Hari thrust his arm deep in a crack between two stones and pulled out a key. He fitted it into the door and turned, hearing a rumble and click as a mechanism worked to open the lock. He did not understand any of this, just knew what his father had taught him. He pushed hard, and the door opened with a squeal of hinges.

The dog smelled food and tried to run past him, but Hari kicked it away.

'Wait,' he said, not bothering to make himself understood any more.

The room that had opened was pitch dark. Hari felt on the floor by the door post, found a flint stone and a twist of cloth and a pan of oil; struck a spark, blew it into flame on the cloth, lit the wick in the oil and a tiny room was revealed. The dog whined with eagerness and fright.

'Quiet, dog.'

He crossed to the far wall and opened a chest lying there. Inside, wrapped in cloth, were strips of dried meat, from rats and cats and dogs, and a few from sheep (animals he had heard of but never seen) stolen from the food carts Company traders stationed at the burrow gates. Hari threw two strips to the dog – rat and cat – and took sheep for himself. He sat and gnawed at the leathery strip, while the dog chewed hungrily, trying to bite off bits small enough to swallow.

'My father found this room, dog. Now he'll never come back.' He drank water from a leather bottle and poured some on the floor for the dog to lap up. 'He stored food and weapons here for his revolution. See the knives and crossbows and spears. Enough for ten men.' Hari laughed. 'Ten men to tear down Company. But he said one day there would be ten hundred. Then ten thousand. Small beginnings in a tiny room – that's what he said. And now he's gone to Deep Salt.'

The dog gave a frightened yelp at the shadowy image appearing in its head. And Hari, too, gave an involuntary yelp of fear. To calm himself he drew Tarl's knife and looked at the blade, tested its sharpness on his thumb. Then he took another strip of meat and cut it into bite-sized chunks and threw them to the dog.

'Don't be afraid, dog. We'll travel together. I need you to sniff out dangers I can't see. But stay with me and you'll eat well.'

He made images of the route he meant to follow through the burrows, out into the wastelands beyond Ceebedee, and into the hills to the north – made images of small imaginary animals he would kill and pools of water they would drink at. Beyond that he could not go. There were deserts, Lo had told him, and mountains and rivers – and what were they? And beyond everything was Deep Salt . . .

The dog rose to its feet with a fearful whine. It slunk towards the door.

'Stay with me, dog,' Hari said softly. 'You're nothing alone. You're food for the rats.'

An image came back from the dog – the pack sleeping after a kill – and Hari said, 'Do you think you can go there? Next time they're hungry they'll tear you apart. How many times have you seen it happen?' He sent the image savagely and the dog howled and turned in a helpless circle, then lay down as though its legs were suddenly weak.

'Yes, dog, you're mine, and I am yours. There's no other way.'

He got up and rummaged through a pile of garments thrown into a corner – trousers, leather jerkins, hooded capes that Tarl had scavenged over the years. He took off his rags and reclothed himself, then filled a satchel with the rest of the meat and the leather bottle with water. Last, he chose a sheath for Tarl's knife and a belt to hang it on. He would take no other weapons – swords and spears were clumsy and he had not learned to use a crossbow, but his knife skills were equal to his father's. The knife and the dog were all he would need. And if he found no animals, the dog would serve as food.

'We'll go through the burrows tonight and sleep in a hole I know beyond Ceebeedee. Then we'll cross the wasteland to the mountains.'

He blew out the lamp, pushed the dog out of the room with his foot, closed the door and hid the key.

'Follow,' he told the dog, 'and don't try to sneak away or my knife will find you.'

Hari started north through the ruins. The dog slunk at his heels with a strip of rat meat in its jaws.

THREE

Radiant Pearl of the Deep Blue Sea, also known as Pearl, rose fully clothed from her bed and crept across the darkened room to her maid, Tealeaf, dozing in a chair.

'It's time to go.'

'Not yet,' Tealeaf said, opening her eyes. 'The doorman isn't sleeping.' She smiled. 'But his eyelids droop. A few more minutes.'

'You can make him sleep. Use the word.'

'Only when I must. Be patient, Pearl. We'll start our journey tonight.'

'And tomorrow they'll hunt me,' Pearl said. 'And capture me and bring me back. Then I'll poison my husband-to-be, and poison myself.'

Tealeaf laughed two notes, like the singing of the glassbird, and said, 'You'll poison no one, child. We'll walk out of here as easily as a butterfly flies. Rest a little more.'

'Don't call me child,' Pearl said. 'I'm old enough to be given in marriage. Cement our two Houses together, my father says, as though I'm a stone to be fixed in a wall, and he, my husband –' she spat the word – 'another stone. You've seen

40

him, Tealeaf. A man who has outlived two wives already, and looks fat enough to have swallowed them whole. I won't – I will not – marry him.'

'No, you will not. You're meant for something else,' Tealeaf said.

'He hunts men in the wastelands for sport, and makes them run from his hounds. And I've heard . . .'

'Enough, Pearl.'

'. . . I've heard if one of his servants spills a drop of soup – one of them did, on his sleeve, and he had the man's hand cut off.'

'Ottmar of Salt is a cruel man. But forget him, Pearl. You're not running away, you're running towards.'

'Yes, to what? I can't stand mysteries.'

Tealeaf stood up from the chair and put her hand on Pearl's brow. 'Go back a little, child. Forget the spoiled daughter of Company. You can put that off like the jewelled cloak you wear to the ball and be the unspoiled young woman you are – and how you've kept her safe I'll never know. But there, you've found her: you are Pearl.'

'If I know my true self it's because of you – what you've taught me,' Pearl said.

'Oh, no. I've simply given you a nudge now and then. You've grown into Pearl by yourself. Now, my dear, the doorman sleeps and we can go. Be quiet in the corridors and, if you must speak, speak in our way.'

'What if someone sees us?'

'Then I'll make him think he hasn't,' Tealeaf said.

Pearl looked at her servant for a moment, wondering at her calmness and the powers she had: things that after all the years of knowing her, and growing from a child into a woman in her care, were still mysterious and frightening. What happened in those parts of Tealeaf made differently from the way humans were made?

'Tealeaf, when we get where we're going, what will happen to me? Will I be like you?'

'Is that what you want?'

'I don't think so. But I don't want to be Radiant Pearl of the Deep Blue Sea, or Tender Blossom in the Dewy Dawn like my sister, or, or . . . Why do they give us these names? Is it to make us think we must only smile and paint ourselves and be what we're not? My brothers can be George and William and Hubert. I'd sooner live in the burrows than be Radiant Pearl – and Ottmar's wife.'

'You'll be neither. Come, Pearl. The doorman sleeps.'

'Do I look all right?' She stepped to the mirror for one last look, and saw in the darkened glass a person she barely recognised, dressed in a brown cape and grey skirt, with a bonnet tied under her chin. She had only seen clothes like this when she went by carriage into Ceebeedee and townswomen stepped out of her way. She could hardly believe she was wearing them and she felt a moment of revulsion, as though these coarse clothes would make her dirty. She could hardly recognise her face either, without painted lips and starred cheeks and her band of pearls across her brow.

'Take your bag,' Tealeaf said, handing it to her – a plain bag of grey cloth with rope handles, and so heavy that Pearl almost dropped it. She had rarely lifted anything heavier than a hand mirror in her life. Yet she was strong – Tealeaf had seen to that, with exercises done secretly in the night that toughened every muscle in her body, and improved her quickness as well, so that, like Tealeaf, she could catch an insect on the wing and study it with sharpened eyes and understand the language of its buzzing. These were skills no other human had; skills no human was aware of. She hoped that on her journey – but where, where were they going? –

Tealeaf would teach her the word that made men fail to see the thing they saw.

'Stop dreaming, Pearl. And stop admiring yourself. It's time to go.'

Tealeaf hefted her own bag, slung it on her back and led the way to the door. It was after midnight. The house was quiet. Pearl's father, Chairman Bowles, and mother, Sweet Stream 'neath the Budding Grove, had retired to their rooms long ago; her sister was sleeping; her brothers were roistering in the town and would not be home until dawn; and the servants had finished their tasks and were sleeping exhausted in their basement dormitory. Hooded lamps made puddles of light in the corridors. The staircase was like a waterfall. Tealeaf went down boldly. She knew where everyone was, and how deeply they slept. The doorman sat snoring on his seat by the door. She went to him quickly, put her hand on his brow and deepened his sleep.

'My father will have him whipped,' Pearl whispered.

'It can't be helped,' Tealeaf said. 'Now quiet, Pearl. I must work harder with the gateman.'

She opened the door quietly, and they stepped into the portico and went down the steps. From there to the gate they walked on the lawn so the gateman in his box would not hear the sound of feet on the lime-chip driveway.

'He's awake,' Tealeaf whispered. She sharpened her eyes and spoke soundlessly. 'Now he stares ahead and will not see. Quickly, Pearl.'

They ran to the box, where the man stood inside with his eyes staring ahead and his mouth hanging as though he had been caught in a yawn.

Tealeaf took the gate key from his belt. She opened the gate and stepped out. Pearl followed.

'He'll be whipped too.'

Tealeaf made no answer. She locked the gate and threw the key over the wall onto the lawn.

'Now, child . . .'

'No. Call me Pearl.'

'Now, Pearl, we must look like hired serving women going home from working at a banquet. Keep your face down like me. Be quick and humble . . .'

'Humble?'

'Unless you want Ottmar for a husband. There are steps further along leading down to the town, and men there who would harm us. Let me deal with them.'

'With the word? If you'd teach me . . .'

'The time will come. Now, by my side, as though we're worn out and anxious for our beds.'

They crossed the broad avenue and found the narrow mouth of a stairway to the town. Pearl turned for a last look at the mansion where she had grown up: the tall roof with the Bowles flag fluttering on top, the windows lit by the moon, the portico, the white driveway and wide lawns. A fountain sparkled. Only two or three mansions were grander than the one where Chairman Bowles and his family lived. She would not miss it. Life there, the endless dressing in gowns, endless painting of her face, the schoolroom where the first lesson taught was the glory of Company and the smaller companies under it, the days of learning dancing and etiquette and the rules of womanly conduct, had been a kind of slavery after the knowledge Tealeaf had revealed to her. She would not miss her family either – her father proud and remote, her mother proud and cruel, and Blossom, her sister, silly and cruel (always slapping her maids), her brothers loudly aggressive, with nothing on their minds, it seemed, but horses and sword-fighting and the pleasures of the town. They spent more on clothes than Blossom did, and almost as much time at the mirror. She would miss none of them. None of them would miss her, except as property to be given in marriage, to the greater glory and profit of their House.

Pearl turned away. She followed Tealeaf down the steps, and although they descended into darkness she felt her heart grow lighter and the weight of all she had learned in her father's house lift from her mind.

She heard Tealeaf whisper like a breeze across her mind: There are two men at the next turning.

What do we do? she answered, in the same way.

They're drunk and slow. We'll be gone before they can move.

They went down lightfooted. One of the men lunged at them and grabbed at Pearl's cloak, but stumbled, cursing, and fell to his knees. The slurred shouts of the other followed them down the steps.

The town came into view, smudged with tavern lights and gas lamps. The buildings of Ceebeedee rose beyond, lit by the moon. Over to the south, stretching to the lights of Port, lay the burrows. Pearl could not believe how wide and far the ruined city stretched, with tumbled roofs catching the light and dead ponds gleaming.

'It's so huge.'

'It was a great city once,' Tealeaf said.

'And people still live there?'

'Thousands of them, in their holes and burrows, living like rats.'

'But Company feeds them.'

'Company sends water carts and food carts when the thirst and hunger grow too much. The burrows are a garden, Pearl, cultivated in its way. When workers in the mines and factories die, the Whips go in and pick some more.'

Pearl shivered. Tealeaf had told her this before but she had never wanted to believe it was true. 'What's that noise?'

'Dogs howling. They're hunting someone. Hurry, Pearl. We must get through the town before dawn. The hunt for us starts then.'

They went down another dozen zigzags and hurried through dark streets towards the fuzz of light and rising clamour of the parts of the town that never slept.

'Can't we go round?' Pearl said.

'There's not enough time. We've got to be at the walls by dawn and find a place to rest for the day. Keep your face down. Say nothing. Do as I do.'

Suddenly they were in a lighted street, with taverns and bars spilling men onto the pavements, and doorways where women leaned, showing their breasts and limbs through clothing artfully disarranged. The doors and alleys led to houses of ill-fame, Pearl supposed, and she could not understand: some of the women were so worn and old. They called out raucously as the two serving women passed by. Men too called after them, making lewd offers and threats, but they kept their eyes lowered modestly and hurried past.

'There,' Tealeaf said as they rounded the corner. 'That's the worst street. It's where the men and women from the slums and factories go.'

'People from the burrows?'

'No. You won't see burrows-people in the town. None are allowed. They offend the eye – have you heard that said?'

'Yes.'

'These are the poor and criminals of your race. Slaves from the burrows aren't free to come and go. They live in barracks at the places where they work.'

'But my father says no one is poor, only lazy. And in the burrows . . .'

'Has he also told you Company cares?'

'Yes, all the time. We feed them. They'd die without us, he says.'

Tealeaf smiled. 'Now isn't the time for lessons, Pearl. Stay in the shadows. No one is safe in these parts.'

It took them another hour to work their way through the district of taverns and gambling dens and brothels. They came to a wealthier part of the town, where the vices and debaucheries were more discreet, but here too they faced insults and threats. A coachman swung his whip at Pearl when she tried to touch his horse, and a powdered and wigged doorman at the entrance of a club shooed them past like stray dogs. In the doorway of another house that Tealeaf said was a casino, Pearl saw her brother Hubert staggering out, supported by a woman in a red velvet cloak and a cat mask. A coach with the Bowles emblem (a hand grasping a lightning bolt) painted on the door drew up, and the coachman helped Hubert and the woman inside.

Pearl kept her face down, although Hubert had not spoken more than a dozen words to her in her life. Hurrying, thinking about her family and how she would not miss them, she almost bumped into a Whip.

'Stop,' the man said softly, taking hold of her with a glove that buzzed like bees. He lifted her face with his other hand. Pearl felt a tingling under her chin. The man's sharp eyes ran over her face. 'It's late to be out. But I think you're not what you seem.'

No one had ever touched Pearl so casually before, or spoken so freely, and she cried, 'How dare you? I'll have you whipped.'

Then she felt a softer pulse than the man's glove on her skin and Tealeaf's voice spoke in her head: Quiet, Pearl. She subsided, but kept the hearing part of her mind open as

Tealeaf turned her speech silently to the Whip: Lower your hand. Close off your sight. You have seen no women passing. You have seen nothing tonight.

The man lowered his glove from Pearl's chin. His eyes grew blank. He stepped away until his back touched a gas-lamp post.

Wait there until we're gone, then go about your rounds. You have nothing to report. Tealeaf took Pearl's arm. 'Come,' she said. 'And never let me hear you talk of whipping again.'

'I'm sorry,' Pearl said. Her chin was still tingling from the man's touch. She wondered what she would have felt if he had turned his gloves to full power.

They went through quieter streets towards Ceebeedee. Few lights showed in the windows of the modest houses where Company's clerks and under-managers lived. The buildings of Ceebeedee showed dark against the moonlit sky. They looked like frogs squatting in a lily pond, as though they might shoot out tongues and eat what they caught. These were the local head offices of the many companies that made a small part of the great one, Company, which had its headquarters around the other side of the world. It was hard for Pearl to understand that her father, so important in the city as head of a great House, would be unimportant if he travelled there. And the buildings, with their marble columns and stairways flowing down to the street, would seem little more than jungle huts to the men who ruled Company from that other place. Yet she felt oppressed by their bulk and squatness, and said to Tealeaf, 'Do we have to go through here?'

'There are watchmen at the doors. We'll use the back streets and try not to be seen.'

They passed through Ceebeedee in that way – alleyways, delivery lanes – and came to a district of warehouses and small factories that Pearl had not known existed. Men still worked in some of them, although dawn had begun to colour the sky. Carts rumbled by, heading for the first pickups of the day, and steam engines heaved and clanked in railyards.

Tealeaf and Pearl slipped by and came to a district of poor housing beside the city walls. There were bars and taverns here too, but they were closed. Tealeaf turned down an alleyway, looking left and right into cottages where women were lighting stoves to start the day. She led Pearl into an archway by the wall and told her to wait. Pearl was exhausted from walking and her arm was aching from the weight of her bag. She slumped down and fell asleep, and dreamed that she was in her own soft bed but someone had put stones in it that hurt her back. She woke with a start as Tealeaf touched her face.

'I've found a room for us. The woman is young and pregnant. Her husband has gone to his job. Say nothing. Keep your face hidden. There should be no need for me to make her forget.'

They went to a tiny cottage at the end of the alley, hidden from the others by an abutment of the wall, and found the woman waiting at the door. She was young, Pearl saw, not much older than her, and thin and poorly clothed, and her pregnancy seemed to cause her pain, for she kept one hand on her belly, but the kitchen she led them into was tidy and clean, and she moved more easily there, putting bread and meat on the table and pouring brown tea into cups. She apologised for the frugal meal.

'It's more than enough,' Tealeaf said. 'We're poor women ourselves.'

The woman looked at Pearl's white hands and silvery nails. 'I don't know who you are. But I'll say nothing. The bed is . . .'

'The bed will be all we need. We'll eat now, and sleep until dark, and be gone before your husband comes home.'

Although Pearl was hungry she had trouble forcing down the dry bread and unseasoned meat. The tea was bitter and made her gag.

'My daughter is tired and unwell,' Tealeaf said. 'She'll use your lavatory, then rest.'

'It's in the yard.'

'Min,' Tealeaf said, inventing the name, 'you go first.'

Pearl obeyed, and could not believe the primitive arrangement – a lean-to, a seat, a can, no more than that. She shuddered with distaste and forced herself to sit. Then she returned to the house and the woman showed her into a room at the back of the kitchen. A basin of water stood on a table beside a bed. Pearl washed.

Tealeaf came in. 'Sleep now, Min.' She turned to the woman. 'We're grateful. Don't wonder who we are. Women run from many things. We're not unusual.'

'When you're gone I'll forget,' the woman said, and Tealeaf smiled.

She laid her hand on the woman's abdomen. 'Your child will be healthy and strong. Now leave us until the sun goes down.'

'Tealeaf,' Pearl said, when the door was closed, 'I can't sleep here. It's their bed and the sheets aren't clean. And look at the pillows . . .'

'It's all they have. Don't make me angry.'

'But look . . .'

'It's how they live. And must live. They work for Company. Now sleep. The bed is narrow, I'll use the floor.'

At once Pearl became contrite: 'No . . .'

'Yes.' Then she smiled. 'I'll sleep as your servant one more time. We're equals after that. And don't worry, Pearl. Dwellers can sleep anywhere.'

'All right. But take a pillow and a blanket. And Tealeaf?'

'Yes?'

'Don't call me Min.' She took off her cape and lay on the bed and was soon asleep.

Tealeaf watched her for a while, a tired look, a sad look on her face. Then she arranged the pillow and blanket on the floor and fell asleep too.

Pearl woke late in the afternoon and did not know where she was. The low ceiling and close walls made it seem she was inside a box. She sat up and opened her mouth to cry out, then saw Tealeaf sleeping on the floor and remembered the room, and that she was Pearl, a daughter who had shamed her family by running away. The punishment if she was caught would be the most severe the law allowed. There would be no marriage, willing or not. Ottmar of Salt would not want her now, but she would be handed over to him, to work as a slavey, or worse, in his household. Similar things had happened to other girls. Pearl had seen them – poor, beaten creatures who cowered even from a kind word.

She looked at her sleeping servant. Only Tealeaf could save her now. But what did saving mean? Where were they going? She was not certain that Tealeaf hadn't worked towards this flight, hadn't chosen her for it all those years ago, rather than Pearl choosing her. She remembered the occasion: her mother leading her into a room where five women stood meekly in a row and telling her she could choose one for herself, and four of them being no different from anyone else's personal maid, while the fifth was a Dweller. She had looked at the woman's hands, three fingered, with a triple-jointed thumb, and shivered at the unnaturalness of it. She had not seen a Dweller before. Then she had looked in her eyes, blue-green eyes with the pupil slitted like a cat's, and felt her gaze entwine with the woman's, and heard a voice

51

whisper in her head: Take me, child, and Pearl had simply raised her hand and pointed.

That had been eight years ago – eight years in which her life had been quietly turned on its head. At first she had been frightened of her servant's eyes and shivered at the touch of her three-fingered hands, but naming her had made things better. 'I'll call you Tealeaf,' she said, and laughed at her own cleverness, and the newly named Tealeaf had smiled: 'Whatever you like.' (It was better than other names girls gave their maids. Pearl knew of one called Slop-bucket.)

Eight years. The main thing Pearl had learned in that time was to keep everything secret. It was secret that Tealeaf taught her about flowers and trees and birds and animals, about all the things that lived in the sea, and how many seas there were and how many lands and how far they stretched, and about Company, how far it stretched, and how it had conquered this land, and how the burrows had been made in the war, and how City had grown and Ceebeedee. None of this knowledge was fit for women and the lives they would lead. Pearl absorbed it and kept quiet. She learned about the stars and the moon and sun, and the clouds and how to read them, and how to read the seasons and the weather. She learned about medicine and her own body, and of cures for sicknesses known to Dwellers but not to humans. She learned to ask questions, endlessly. The only ones Tealeaf would not answer were about herself and the land where her people lived.

'We're ordinary. We aren't known for anything special,' she said.

'But you can speak,' Pearl said.

That was the main secret: Tealeaf could speak silently and be heard in someone's head. Slowly, with great care, over several years, she taught Pearl how to do it – to speak and hear.

'But I could do it right from the start,' Pearl said. 'I heard you say: "Take me".'

'Yes, you could,' Tealeaf said. It was all she would say. And it was only after several more years that she let Pearl see how she could make people move or hold them still, and then make them forget what they had heard and seen.

'Teach me,' Pearl demanded.

'When you're ready,' Tealeaf said.

I need to know now, Pearl whispered to herself, looking down at her servant's sleeping face, so I can help us escape.

She rose quietly from the bed, stepped over Tealeaf and crossed the room to the door. The pregnant woman was sitting in a chair by the kitchen window, using the light to sew a collar on a shirt. She put down her work, rose to her feet and made as if to curtsey.

'No, please don't. Don't do that,' Pearl said. 'I'm like you.'

The woman smiled. 'Then do my sewing for me. Chop me an onion for the stew.'

'I can't – I . . .'

'You're not like me. Please, can I see your hand?'

Pearl held one out and the woman took it. 'So soft. Look at mine.'

'Yes. I'm sorry.'

'Who are you?'

'My name is Pearl.'

The woman smiled. 'Not Min?'

'No. That was a lie. I'm running away from a marriage I don't want. To a man who is cruel and old and ugly.'

'What's his name?'

'Ottmar of Salt.'

The woman shivered. 'My husband works in one of his warehouses. He stacks sacks of salt fourteen hours a day. And

Ottmar sends orders that they must work harder. Where will you run to?'

'I don't know.'

'You can stay here. We'll hide you.'

'No, my mother . . .'

'She's not your mother. I've seen her eyes.'

'And I've seen yours,' Tealeaf said from the bedroom door, 'and I know you're honest and kind. We're grateful for your offer, but it would put you in danger – you and your husband. And your child. We have a destination. Tilly – is that your name?'

'How did you know?'

Tealeaf did not answer. 'You know who Pearl is and what they'll do to her if she's caught. So we're going – somewhere else. They'll be hunting us now, but we've come this far without being seen and we'll be gone before it's dark. When Whips come searching . . .'

'Whips will come?' Tilly said in fright.

'My father will pay for a search, for his honour. Ottmar too. They'll go everywhere in the city,' Pearl said.

'But no one has seen us in this street,' Tealeaf said. 'They'll ask. You'll say no. Can you do that?'

'Yes,' Tilly whispered.

'Then you're safe. Soon it will be dark. If you'll let us eat some of your stew . . .?'

'I've made enough,' Tilly said. She put two plates on the table.

'No, my dear, three plates. Eat with us, but not so much you can't eat again with your husband.'

Tilly served the stew. It was rag-end meat, full of gristle and fat, but Pearl ate because she was hungry. She was thankful there had been no time to put onions in.

Darkness fell and Tilly lit a candle. Pearl and Tealeaf

fetched their bags from the bedroom.

'I have nothing I can give you as a parting gift,' Tilly said.

'You're giving us your silence. That's a gift. And Pearl has a guest gift for you.'

'Yes,' Pearl said. She felt in her bag and drew out a handful of coins that lay on the bottom. She put them in Tilly's hand. 'A gift, not a payment,' she said. 'I'm sorry it's so small.'

'But it's more,' Tilly stammered, 'more than my husband earns in half a year.'

'I keep it for trinkets and sweetmeats,' Pearl said, feeling ashamed.

'Now, Tilly,' Tealeaf said, 'we'll go out through the back yard and along by the wall. And you will try to forget you saw us.'

Tilly tried to curtsey again, but Pearl stopped her and kissed her cheek. Then she and Tealeaf slipped away.

They went out by a little gate beside the lavatory and moved along silently at the back of a warehouse. The wall cutting City off from the wasteland rose on their left, a dozen body lengths high and a body length wide. A narrow half-forgotten gate was set in an alcove, where a gateman sat dozing at the end of his shift with his back against the wall. A newly lit gas lamp burned above him.

Tealeaf leaned close.

'Sir.'

The man's eyes flew open. 'Hey,' he began.

Tealeaf fixed him with her eyes: Say nothing, she said. Stand up.

The man obeyed, with the same glassy look Pearl had seen in the mansion gateman.

Take your key and open the gate.

He obeyed again, moving clumsily. The gate creaked open. Pearl and Tealeaf slipped through.

Now lock the gate. Put the key back in your belt. No one has passed this way. You have seen no women. Go back to your dreaming.

He followed each command. Pearl felt she could see memory slide from his mind and flit away into the dark like a bat.

'Tealeaf, when can I learn to do that?'

'Perhaps never. Now be quiet while I think which way to go.'

'You didn't make Tilly forget.'

'She was a friend. We've got two hours before the moon comes up. We'll have to be out in the scrub by then or the wall patrol will see us. Come, quickly. None are close now.'

'Tealeaf.'

'What?'

'The search hasn't come here yet or the gateman would have been awake.'

'Ah, you noticed. You're learning to be a fugitive.'

They travelled away from City across stony ground. Out beyond the first jumble of rocks they took off their capes and skirts and replaced them with jerkins and trousers. They changed the shoes they had worn through the streets for soft leather boots. Their bags were no lighter because they must leave nothing behind for horsemen and their sniffer dogs to find, but Tealeaf refolded them, changing them into packs that would sit comfortably on their backs.

'Now, Pearl, we go hard. We need to be in the hills by dawn.'

Pearl had never walked so far or fast. Her feet grew sore, her legs ached, her breathing grew ragged, but when she begged to rest Tealeaf answered abruptly: 'You can sleep in the daytime. Night is all we have.'

'Tealeaf . . .'

'Do you want to spend your life as a slave in Ottmar's house?'

That kept her moving. Once they stopped and crouched unmoving while Tealeaf sent out sharp spears of thought at a hunting fangcat, half as tall as a horse, and drove him back and sent him spitting on his way.

'If you'd teach me I could help,' Pearl said.

'Soon, Pearl. Soon.'

'Does it hurt?' Pearl said, hearing the tiredness in her voice.

'An animal so savage – it's like pushing on a door that won't close.'

The moon slid across the sky, shining so brightly it threw black shadows like hour-hands out to the travellers' sides. City shrank to a pencil line on the horizon and jumbled hills grew large across a shallow river that shone as yellow as butter. They crossed, wading up to their knees. Far away, they heard the fangcat take his morning prey.

'That sounded like a person,' Pearl said, shivering.

'No, a goat, coming down to drink at the river. Others are coming now, do you see? They know the cat has taken what it needs.'

Pearl saw animals picking their way down from the hills. The sky was turning pink in the dawn.

'Are there fangcats in the hills?'

'I don't know. There are worse things behind.'

Pearl looked back but could see nothing. She emptied water out of her boots and put them on again, then trudged after Tealeaf over scurfy ground, through spiky grass. The hills rose almost as steeply as a wall. Tealeaf found a way up, turning between boulders and scrambling on goat tracks. They climbed for an hour, then turned for a last look over the wasteland. The sun had coloured it golden and picked out

City beyond. The moon, faded to silver, was sinking below the faraway hill where the Bowles mansion, the Ottmar mansion and all the other great houses stood. Pearl could not pick them out. They're nothing, she decided; but, in her exhaustion, thought longingly of her comfortable bed, and also, in her hunger, of the breakfast Tealeaf brought her each morning on a tray.

Tealeaf would not serve her now, not in that way.

'We'll sleep here,' Tealeaf said, putting down her pack in the shade of a boulder.

'What if they use dogs to track us?'

'Confusing dogs is one of the easier things.'

Pearl stayed where she was, looking at City and the squat jumble of Ceebeedee. The dark stain of the burrows spread out to the south, with the sea shining white beyond it. East, and far away, smoke rose from the chimneys of the factory towns where workers stolen from the burrows spent their lives in slave labour. That, at least, was what Tealeaf had taught her – one of the secrets she kept. She could not imagine their lives. How could anyone be poorer than Tilly, who was not even a burrows-woman? She hoped that Tilly would be safe.

Pearl began to turn away. Then she saw a movement on the golden plain – something shapeless, moving fast, leaving a cloud of dust. It took her a moment to work out what it was.

'Tealeaf. Horses.'

Tealeaf ran to her side. 'Yes. From City. Hunting us. But now they're chasing something else. See.'

Pearl made out a figure in front of the horsemen, running towards the river, with something – a dog, was it? – loping at its side.

'What are they doing?'

'It's a burrows-man and a dog. Our hunters are hunting

him.' She peered harder with her cat-like eyes. 'He's a boy.'

'Can we save him?'

'There's no way. He'll get to the river ahead of them, and get across, but they'll catch him before he reaches the hills.'

'What will they do?'

'Kill him.'

'Stop the horses. Push them back like you pushed the fangcat.'

'I can't. It's too far. Even at the foot of the hills it will be too far. Come away, Pearl.'

'How do you know he's from the burrows?'

'He has brown skin.'

'Do burrows-people have that?'

'Yes. A brown-skinned race. Come away.'

The boy reached the river. He scooped the dog in his arms and waded across, then threw the animal down and ran again. The horsemen reached the river and milled about.

'Tealeaf,' Pearl cried, 'it's Hubert, my brother. See his dappled horse. He's hunting me.'

'But he doesn't let it get in the way of his sport. See, they're handing him his lance. He will make the kill.'

Hubert, on his dappled stallion, rode high-stepping across the river. The Bowles emblem fluttered at the head of his lance. He spurred his mount onto dry land and closed quickly on the boy. Pearl watched in horror. She tried to scream out to him to stop, but no sound came from her mouth.

The boy looked over his shoulder and stopped running. He turned and faced the horseman, who lowered his lance-point for the kill. He spurred the horse and it leaped forward. Then it whinnied suddenly, and shied and stumbled, throwing Hubert from the saddle. A puff of dust floated up from the place where he landed. He rolled on the ground, then came to his knees – and the boy, instead of running, stood and waited.

Tealeaf had made a small cry as the horse shied. She fixed her eyes on the boy, watching every move.

'My brother,' Pearl cried. 'He's not hurt, he's getting up.' She did not know if she was sorry or glad. 'He's getting his sword out. He's going to kill him.'

Hubert advanced, his blade flashing in the sun. The boy waited. The black and yellow dog cowered at his side.

'Stop him, Tealeaf.'

'I can't. But I think Hubert doesn't know who he's fighting with.'

As she spoke the boy moved. His hand came up so quickly Pearl could not see where his weapon had come from: a knife, with a blade that gleamed like coal. Hubert was running at him with his sword held two-handed, pointing like a spear. The boy took a single step, raised his arm and threw. The knife blinked twice as it sped the dozen paces to the man. The blade took him in the throat and sank in to the hilt. Hubert fell.

Pearl felt as if she had been stabbed. She stood swaying. 'My brother,' she whispered. Her hand went to her throat as if to stem a flow of blood. Tealeaf moved close and put her arm around her.

The boy walked to the body. He spat on it. Then he withdrew the knife and wiped the blade on Hubert's jacket. The dog approached and sniffed at the blood. The boy kicked it away. He raised the knife and slashed it at the men beyond the river. They replied with a shout, and began to cross. The boy turned to call the dog who was lapping at Hubert's throat, and the pair ran towards the hills.

'They're safe now,' Tealeaf said.

'He killed my brother,' Pearl whispered.

'To stop your brother killing him.'

The horsemen surged up from the river and spurred their

horses. Several stopped at Hubert's body and jumped down, but rose at once and shook their spears at the running boy. The others galloped after him, shrieking their battle cry, 'Bowles and Company', which had always seemed comical to Pearl when she heard it in military processions. Now it had a blood-thirsty, half-crazy sound.

The boy reached the jumbled boulders well out of spear range, but several of the horsemen had drawn bolt guns from their saddles. The shots shone like yellow stars falling towards him. He threw himself behind a boulder, with the dog scrambling at his heels. The horsemen milled. One or two jumped from their mounts and hunted in the narrow spaces between the rocks, guns held ready, while others threw their spears randomly or fired bolts that pocked the stone with smoking holes – but the boy was gone. Pearl and Tealeaf glimpsed him climbing, fast and sure, heaving the dog now and then in places it couldn't climb. Soon he was out of range of both spears and guns.

Hubert's horse had galloped free and several of his company set off in pursuit. Others scanned the cliffs.

'They've seen us,' Tealeaf said.

Shouts drifted up. Pearl could not make out the words but guessed they would be about dishonour and death.

'Now they'll catch us,' she said.

'No. These aren't men who go on foot. They'll take your brother home. After that there'll be a search, but we'll be gone. Take your pack again. We'll go further on and find a safer place.'

Pearl did not move. Tealeaf saw her horror and confusion at her brother's death, mixed with fear for herself. 'I'm sorry,' she said, then silenced her tongue and spoke in the way that was natural to her. Pearl heard the voice whisper in her head: Your brother's dead, and grief is natural, even though you didn't love him, Pearl. But he lived the life he chose and died the way such men die, and he's gone. Remember, if you can, what was good. Come now, Pearl, come my child. We must leave here and make ourselves safe. Then, when we've slept, we must find the boy.

The voice was comforting and soothing, like a balm, like a hand stroking her brow, until those last words, which struck like a hand slapping her face.

'No,' she cried. 'Why do we have to find him? He killed my brother.'

Be calm, Pearl. Make yourself still. We have long ways to go and much to do.

'Why? Why find him?'

'Because,' Tealeaf said, using normal speech, 'we must. Pearl, do you think your brother's horse threw him without a reason?'

'What?'

'The boy spoke. I couldn't hear what he said, but he spoke to the horse.'

'That's impossible.'

'I would have thought so. But I heard something. A whisper. And the horse shied. And now I must find the boy and speak to him.'

'Why?'

'I thought you were the only one, Pearl. The only one I've found in all my years in the city. But now, it seems, there's another.'

'Another what?'

Tealeaf spoke silently: That, my dear, is what we must find out.

FOUR

Hari threw a strip of meat to the dog and took one himself. They ate on a rock ledge overlooking the plain. Two horsemen led the dappled stallion back to where the dead man lay, and others hefted him across the saddle, tying him so he wouldn't slide off.

'I'm sorry you didn't have time to eat him, dog,' Hari said. The men no longer bothered him. He was out of range of their bolt guns and they would not risk climbing on the steep paths. He was more worried about the two women in men's clothes he had glimpsed watching him as he scrambled up. They might have men with them who would be dangerous.

He drank from his bottle, then held water in his cupped hand for the dog.

Keep watching, dog. And keep sniffing with your nose. There are people.

The dog wagged its tail without pausing in its lapping. Hari had grown used to receiving no answer except tiredness, fear, and now and then an uncertain gratitude. He must try to make the animal more confident, and stronger too, or it would be no use to him. It had given no warning in the dawn that horsemen approached, and with its lame foot it had slowed their running. He wondered if it would be better to kill it for food. The dog caught the thought and leaped away.

'No, dog,' Hari said. 'I won't kill you. You're something to talk to. But we'll have to find food soon, and water. One more day, that's all we've got.'

He put the bottle in his pack and stood up, and could not resist shouting at the men below: 'Death to Company.' He untied his trousers and pissed at them down the cliff face. One or two raised their guns but did not fire. Hari looked around for the women but they had gone.

'Time to get out of here, dog,' he said. 'Shift yourself.'

They climbed again, then walked in gullies and dry creek beds. At noon they found a shallow cave and slept. There had been no sight or sound of pursuit and no evidence of people living in these hills. As for the women, Hari did not think they would follow him. Something in the way they had stood made him think they were running too.

He woke late in the afternoon. He was worried about food and water. The stream beds stayed dry and he had seen no sign of animals.

Find me a goat, dog. Find a sheep, he said.

They went on until dark, slept again, then travelled by the light of the moon. When the sun came up Hari saw mountains in the distance. They were black with trees at the base and white on top. That must be snow. Lo had told him of snow. If he could get that far, to the trees, there would be water, and animals to hunt and maybe fruit he could pick. But the mountains were far off and the dry yellow hills went on and on.

They ate the last meat and drank the last water. Hari tried not to think of killing the dog. He stopped in a bare gully where a stream might run in the wet months and tried digging with his knife, but the sand and pebbles stayed dry. A few small bushes with spiky leaves grew on the slopes, but they grew no fruit and the leaves were bitter when he tasted them.

'Come on, dog. We've got to get to the mountains.'

They came out of the gully. The land ahead was flatter, sloping upwards gradually. There were outcrops of silvery rock and isolated boulders tall as houses. The mountains seemed further away now that the sun was high. Deep Salt lay somewhere beyond – maybe far beyond. Hari began to understand how hopeless his journey was. But nothing would make him give up. He set his eyes on the highest peak and trudged on.

The dog was ranging out to one side. Suddenly it stopped and gave a soft bark. It sniffed one way, then the other, and set off eagerly, its nose to the ground. Hari followed.

'A goat,' he whispered. 'Let it be a goat.'

They rounded a low hill and the plain opened out again. The dog stopped. Far away something moved slowly – a brown dot among the isolated trees. For a moment Hari could not make out what it was. Then the dot grew larger – from a shape crouching into a person standing – and he saw it was one of the women he had glimpsed as he made his escape from the horsemen. The taller one. She crouched to dig with her hands, gathered something, moved on, dug again.

'Dog,' Hari whispered, 'you've found something here.'

If he couldn't hunt a goat he would hunt the woman. She carried a bag and put whatever she dug into it. It could only be food. He would take it – kill her and get the food. And if the dog could not eat whatever she was gathering, then it could feed on her body.

The dog, understanding, gave a whimper of anticipation. It started forward, and Hari followed, stepping softly. They passed an outcrop of rocks, rising like broken walls from the dusty ground, and the dog stopped suddenly, taking a new scent. It circled, confused, then pointed with its nose.

'What is it?' Hari whispered. 'Something in the rocks?' Perhaps it was a goat, a deer – or the other woman. He drew his knife.

The dog, low to the ground, crept into the shady side of the outcrop and froze. Hari followed, crouching, knife held ready. A foot came into view, an outflung leg, a leg bent up, then a jerkined torso, then a face, a white face, side on, with eyes closed and mouth slightly open. Hari could not believe his luck: a City woman, Company woman. Sleeping. An easy kill. He heard her sigh and breathe.

He moved closer. Her head was pillowed on a bag. There would be food inside.

Closer.

He saw she was little more than a girl. It did not stop him.

Tealeaf and Pearl had heard the boy shout at the men on the plain and saw him piss down the cliff at them.

'He's a savage boy. We'll have to be careful,' Tealeaf said.

They waited until he and the dog had gone, then made their way to the rock ledge where they had stood. Below them, the Bowles horsemen were riding in a dejected band across the river. Hubert's body, wrapped in a cloak, was tied across the saddle. Pearl said goodbye to her brother silently. She imagined her father's rage and grief. Hubert had been the oldest son, bred to lead Bowles in its expansion. Now there were only the stupid ones, William and George. She turned away.

'This boy leaves an easy trail,' Tealeaf said.

'I can't see it.'

'Smell it, Pearl. He smells of hatred.'

Pearl tried to open her mind, sliding it through her senses, and seemed at last to catch a smell like something going bad at the back of a shelf.

'Yes,' Tealeaf said, 'we follow that.'

They set off carefully, but soon Pearl let the scent fade, left it to Tealeaf, and used her eyes instead, trying to pick out footmarks on the ground.

'He's going fast. Heading for the mountains,' Tealeaf said.

'I can't see mountains. Is that where we're going?'

'Yes. Two more days.'

They followed, although the boy was out of sight. When his scent spread into a pool, they knew he was resting. They retreated, found shade and rested too. Pearl slept, then they started again, following the boy's pattern. Pearl thought she saw mountains gleaming in the distance, but lost them as she and Tealeaf walked through shallow gullies. In the morning the peaks stood tall and clear, and further off than she had expected. She lost heart.

'Do we have to catch him?'

'Not yet a while. We can go ahead and wait. I'll have to gather food. We're running out. Food for him too. He won't know how to find it out here.'

They moved off to one side, then ahead of where the boy must be, keeping downwind so the dog wouldn't take their scent. At midday Tealeaf said, 'Rest, Pearl.' She pointed to a strip of shade narrow against the foot of rocks. 'Call if you need me. I won't be far away.'

'What food can you find out here?'

'You'll see. Try to sleep.'

Pearl lay down, using her pack as a pillow. It made her jealous that Tealeaf seemed more concerned for the boy they followed than for her. She did not seem to realise what Pearl was suffering: loss of her brother, loss of her home. Images of her old life played in her mind – food and soft eiderdowns and clothes and entertainments – then she thought of Tilly, who had sheltered them and fed them, and gradually her tiny house and well-used bed became the place she would choose to be. It seemed warmer and more comfortable, with Tilly stirring stew in a blackened pot at the stove . . .

After a few moments Pearl slept without dreaming, but soon a disturbance crept in from one side – an eddying of mud in the still water of her sleep. It grew and had a smell and shape, and something hard and sharp reached out from it, turning its point, seeking her. She woke with a gasp. The boy stood over her, holding a black-bladed knife. His face was filled with hatred; his eyes burned like the fangcat's they had met on the plain. He reached for her, to hold her still and plunge the knife.

Pearl said, 'Stop,' and he did not.

She swam underneath her terror, looking for a word, and found it – any word, as long as she spoke it, thought it, in the right way.

Stop, she commanded, soundlessly.

It was almost right. He jerked his head to one side as if avoiding something thrown at him. Stepped back, shook himself, looked at her with fear and calculation. He stepped further away, four steps, and raised his knife to throw.

'Be still,' Pearl said, firmer now, finding the source more easily.

He gasped and seemed to fight a creature that had leaped at him and fastened on; tried to push it, stab it. 'No,' he screamed.

Stop, Pearl said silently. It was easier silent.

He panted and fell still, and slowly his eyes began to glaze as she had seen the gateman's and the Whip's when Tealeaf commanded.

Put down your knife.

He bent in a drugged way and laid it on the ground. Behind him the dog began to howl.

Be quiet, Pearl commanded.

She stood up and gathered her pack. Now what do I do? she thought. She had no idea how long she could hold the boy, or if she could stop him again if he woke.

Go, she told him, run away as fast as you can. Never come back.

He began to shake his head and punch the heel of his palm against his temple, as though to shake something out.

Go away, she commanded.

But this time her voice seemed to waken, not hold him, and the layer of drugged sleep began to move slowly off the surface of his eyes. He reached for the knife.

Don't touch it, she said. Leave it there.

His hand slowed as though he were forcing it through tar, but he pushed – she heard him push with his mind.

Be still, she said.

He answered her – words like an insect scratching in a paper bag: You can't stop me. I'm stronger than you.

Stay still, she replied.

I'll kill you, he said. Then he spoke aloud: 'How long do you think you can hold me, girl? In a moment you'll be too tired. Then . . .'

Be quiet, she said, and saw him jerk with surprise at the strength of the command. But he wrenched his eyes away from her and forced his hand down again to pick up the knife.

Leave it, she said, more quietly. Step back. Go away.

No, he replied. I'll wait. And you'll step back, and I will kill you. He spoke aloud: 'Company dies. You saw me kill the horseman. All of you will die.'

She struck him with her mind, visualising it – a hand-slap with a dozen times her natural strength, drawing power from a source she had no time to understand – and the boy reeled back, almost standing on the dog. He looked at her and gave an ugly grin.

'You can't do that again. You've used up your strength.' Then he changed his attack. She heard him make the command: Bite her, dog.

The animal slunk at her.

Stop, dog. Lie still, she said.

With a whine of bewilderment, it obeyed.

The boy grinned again. 'We can do this all day. And in the end I'll win. I am stronger.'

Pearl did not believe him; she was stronger – but he was right; he would win because she had made commands that exhausted her, and now she could barely keep awake.

Pick up your knife and throw it away, she said.

He jerked his head again as though she'd slapped him, then obeyed: he picked up the knife. But instead of throwing it he turned to face her.

'My father's knife makes me strong,' he said. He took a step back to get his distance, and although she cried: Stop, then cried it aloud, he balanced the knife in his hand and raised his arm. He drew back his shoulder to throw.

'That's enough, boy,' Tealeaf said.

He swung around. Tealeaf was standing beside the furthest wall of rock, and seemed to Pearl almost as tall. The boy was not afraid.

'Two to kill,' he said, and set himself to throw again.

Stop, Tealeaf said, and Pearl heard the difference from her own commands. This was effortless, and closed the boy down like the setting sun. Tealeaf could leave him there forever if she chose, leave him standing like a statue beside the rocks.

The dog howled and ran.

Come back, dog, Tealeaf said. No one will hurt you.

She walked past the boy, taking no notice of him, and put her hand on Pearl's brow.

'Cold,' she said. 'You've used yourself up.'

'He was going to kill me,' Pearl whispered.

'Yes, I felt him. I came as fast as I could.'

'I stopped him.'

'I felt that too. You've found it, Pearl.'

'The word?'

'There is no word. There's a way. He has it too. But both of you are children, you're like buckets full of holes, spilling your strength everywhere.'

'I can't help it,' Pearl said. She felt tears running down her face. 'If I hadn't pushed him back . . .'

'Yes, you did well. And now you're tired. You need to sleep.'

'Send him away first.'

'No, we'll keep him. Don't be afraid, he'll be asleep too.' She said to the boy: Lie down over there in the shade. Sleep until I tell you to wake.

He turned with stiff movements, and lay down and closed his eyes.

Let go of your knife, Tealeaf said.

He unclosed his fingers and the knife slid to the ground. Tealeaf picked it up.

'You too, Pearl.'

'I don't need you telling me.'

She moved as far from the boy as the shade allowed, arranged her pack, rested her head on it and slept at once. This time she dreamed. It was peaceful at first, with a peace greater than any she had ever known: landscapes of hill and mountain, the hills golden and the mountains blue. She drifted

71

over them, and floated down long flanks of bush and gully to the sea, where rivers emptied, staining the blue with green, and long low waves turned over on themselves and ran foaming on beaches of yellow sand. One moment Pearl hovered over them; the next she was sweeping away, almost as high as the clouds. Far below white birds dived at schools of fish, which slid sideways with a silver flash as they escaped. The sun shone. A breeze touched her face. Pearl, she said, my name is Pearl, and she felt the knowledge of who she was open like a flower. Her mind became still in the glow and harmony of it: she was Pearl. She had never known such certainty before.

She slept on and the dream faded and nothing disturbed her for good or bad during a time that, when it ended, seemed to have lasted her whole life. Then she turned – turned over in the shade of the rock – and dreamed again – and now suddenly the fish were torn and the birds had blood on their beaks, and here, suddenly too, people were running on the beach and falling on their knees, and horsemen with lances galloped after them and over them. People fell. Women and children fell. The sand turned red. She writhed in it, screaming as a black sword fell on her. It seemed to strike, but turned into a hand that rested on her brow. She heard a voice murmur: Easy, child – Tealeaf's voice. Sleep without dreaming. She obeyed, but felt too, before the black sweet nothingness came down, that she was obeying herself.

Stars were shining when she woke, and fading as the moon came up. Tealeaf was sitting by a small fire, with the dog sleeping beside her. A pannikin of water steamed on the embers. Pearl watched, remembering her dreams. She did not think Tealeaf had given them to her, but suspected Tealeaf knew.

'Where did you get the wood?' she said.

'They're twigs from the ironwood tree. They burn for hours.'

'You must have been here before.'

'I've been many places, Pearl. Come and drink some tea.'

'I didn't think we brought tea.'

'We didn't. It's from the ironwood, from the leaves. You'll find it bitter at first but sweet later on.'

Pearl sipped it and made a face, but found a faint honey taste after a while.

'Did he have dreams too?' she said, nodding at the sleeping boy.

'Worse ones. He's seen worse things, Pearl.'

'Do we have to wake him?'

'Soon. He'll be hungry. The dog was hungry.'

'He talked to the dog. He talked to me.'

'Yes, I know.'

'Is that why we have to keep him?'

Tealeaf sighed. 'Wait a while, Pearl. I'll tell you later. Finish your tea. I'll cook some food.' She pulled her bag towards her and lifted out a handful of white grubs, some as long as her thumb.

'What are those?' Pearl cried.

'Muggy grubs, from the Muggy moth. They grow in the ironwood roots. We're lucky it's the season for them.'

'I'm not eating grubs.'

'Then you'll go hungry. I've taken off their heads and squeezed the poison out. The dog likes them.'

Pearl wondered if she had killed them while she was having her dream of birds tearing fish apart. She watched while Tealeaf placed them carefully in the embers, and soon a smell like roasting meat reminded her how hungry she was.

'Help yourself, Pearl. I'm not your maid any more.' Tealeaf tossed a raw grub to the dog, who snapped it hungrily out of the air.

Pearl hooked a grub from the embers and put it to cool

73

on a flat piece of rock. She tasted it and found it more sweet than savoury, and with a spicy after-taste.

'How do you know about these things, Tealeaf?'

'Eat some more. I want to wake Hari, then I'll tell you.'

'Who's Hari? Oh, him. Do you expect me to forget he killed my brother?'

'I expect you to remember that your brother was going to kill him. Now eat, and leave some for him. And, Pearl . . .'

'Yes?'

'When I do wake him, remember your dream.'

Pearl ate another grub.

Which part of the dream, she wondered, the good part or the bad?

Hari's dream took him to places so dark and violent and bloody that even he, used to violence and blood, closed his eyes and wailed in terror. He tried to turn and run, but the dream was on his back, and bursting from the ground at his feet and swooping from above – things that crawled and killed, things that flew and killed, in humped and clawed and crooked shapes, yet with men inside them. They had faces that he knew, and all of them a second face, hiding behind. He tried to turn his eyes away, but everywhere the creature sprang into life, advancing, locked into itself, wearing its contorted face, and his face too. He wept and wailed and turned and ran, but met himself everywhere. He cowered and fell to his knees and hid his eyes. A weight came down and crushed him. And slowly, under it, his terror faded until a tiny squeak of pain was all he could make. That sound faded too, the pain faded, and a thin whisper took its place: Hari, Hari, Hari, there are places still to go. It sank into blackness, and Hari sighed and rolled over, and nothing was the sum of all he knew.

He slept a long while without dreaming.

Then a whisper started: his name again, but this time with a friendly sound. It raised him from a stillness so deep and so enfolding he felt it rolling off like water, and he was walking on grass, among trees – grass greener than he had ever seen and trees so tall they touched the sky. A stream flowed by. Sand gleamed silver on the bottom. Small fish swam. He wondered how he was able to recognise things he had never seen. The voice said: Hari, there are many things to know. He stood still. For hours he stood still, among the trees, by the stream, with his hands easy by his sides and his eyes seeing without knowledge or thought, and a space opening inside him . . .

A new voice spoke in his ear: Hari, wake up. It's time to eat.

He woke and sat up, and looked at the woman and the girl by the fire.

'Who are you?' he said to the woman.

'My name is Tealeaf,' she said.

'What are you?'

'Another person, but from another place, and so a little different from you.'

'The girl is Company. That's why I've got to kill her.'

'Not now. Not ever. Come to the fire, Hari. Come and eat.' She smiled. 'Perhaps you had bad dreams because you're hungry.'

'I had another dream – and not a bad one.'

'Perhaps that too came because you're hungry.' She threw something to the dog, who snapped it and swallowed. 'Muggy grubs. There are plenty left.'

'Come here, dog,' Hari said.

The animal rose, whining.

'Go on, dog,' Tealeaf said. 'You're with him.'

The girl said, 'You can't kill me without your knife.'

'I can do it with my hands,' Hari said.

'No more talk of killing,' Tealeaf said. 'Come and eat. Then we'll decide what to do.'

Hari stood up and went to the fire. He sat down opposite Tealeaf.

'There are grubs roasting. Help yourself,' she said.

Hari took a stick and hooked one out of the embers. It burned his tongue and he spat it into his hand.

'Manners,' said the girl.

'What's her name?' Hari said.

'Ask her,' Tealeaf said.

'I don't talk to Company.'

'I'm not,' said the girl. 'My brother was. You killed him.'

'Was he the one on the horse?' He put the grub in his mouth and chewed with enjoyment.

'What did you tell the horse?' Tealeaf said.

'I told him to watch out for the spitting snake.'

'So he shied, and Hubert fell. Where did you learn to talk to horses?'

Hari took another grub from the embers and tossed it from hand to hand, letting it cool. 'I need some water,' he said.

Tealeaf handed him a leather bottle. 'That's the last. I'll show you how to find more.'

'Show me too,' the girl said.

Hari saw she was jealous. He grinned at her. 'Your brother was a fool. Company men are easy to kill.' But as he spoke something jagged at him, like a thorn catching his skin. He could not tell whether it came from the woman, Tealeaf, trying to control him, from the look of pain in the girl's eyes, or whether it started in himself, from his dream. He drank from the bottle, hiding his confusion.

'It was a fair fight,' he said.

'Horses,' Tealeaf said. 'And dogs. How did you learn to talk to them?'

'Easy,' Hari said.

'And people? You could speak with me if you wanted to. You spoke with Pearl.'

'Is that her name? A Company name.'

'How?'

Hari looked into her eyes. The slitted upright pupils made him blink. He handed the bottle back into her three-fingered hand. Lo had told him once . . .

'You're a Dweller.'

Lo had never met one; had not even been sure they existed, any more than salt tigers existed. None had been seen in the burrows. But Tealeaf was real – eyes and hands, and skin red in the firelight – and Hari knew she could take whatever knowledge she wanted from him. He tried to remember if there had been Dwellers in his dream.

'We'll talk about me later on,' Tealeaf said. She reached into the bag at her side. 'Take your knife.'

'No,' Pearl cried.

'Quiet, Pearl.' Tealeaf handed the black-bladed knife across the fire. 'He needs it. You don't feel whole without a knife, do you, Hari?'

'No,' Hari whispered, taking it. He had not expected to see the knife again.

'Especially this one. Why this, Hari?'

'It was my father's.'

'Did you know it's a Dweller knife? See the ridges in the handle. They're made for three fingers. Where did your father get it?'

'He found it one day in Blood Burrow.'

'It's very old. Dwellers visited the city when it was called

77

Belong. After that, after Company came . . .' She shrugged and fell quiet.

Hari fingered the knife, felt the balance, tested the blade. A single flick would send it across the fire into the girl's throat. But the thought came without energy and turned back on itself and was lost.

Tealeaf sighed. She put another handful of twigs on the fire and pushed more grubs under them. 'Eat some more, both of you. Then we'll find some water.'

'I learned by myself at first,' Hari said. 'Then I learned from an old man called Lo. He was blind. But he had lived a long time and had a long time to learn.'

'Were there any others?'

'Just me and Lo. I can talk to dogs and cats and rats. Horses too. And sometimes my father could hear and whisper back. No one else, until her. Until . . . Pearl.'

'I'm better at it,' Pearl said. 'I stopped you killing me.'

'I would have got you, if she hadn't come,' Hari said. 'But you needn't be scared, I'm not going to now.'

'I'm not scared.'

The dog whimpered, and Tealeaf said, 'Children quarrel. I don't want children with me. There are mountains to cross. Tell me, Hari, where are you running to?'

'I'm not running. Company took Tarl, my father. I'm going to set him free.'

'Where did they take him?'

'Deep Salt.'

'Ah,' Tealeaf said. She smiled at Hari. 'Do you know where that is?'

'Lo said north. So I'm going north.'

'So are we.'

'To Deep Salt?'

'In that direction. Travel with us, Hari.'

78

'Nobody asks me,' Pearl complained.

'I think we'll need each other, Pearl,' Tealeaf said. 'There's dangerous country ahead, and danger behind. And much to learn. The first is . . .?'

'Water,' Hari said, and he grinned as Pearl, not to be left out, repeated it.

They ate the last grubs, then, as the moon came up, threw dirt on the fire. When they set out, Hari and the dog came last. He saw it made the girl nervous having him behind her, but he wanted to stay at the back and see how Tealeaf found her way. His dreams still troubled him. He did not think they had come by accident, but wasn't sure that the woman, the Dweller, had put them in his head. Perhaps she had simply opened something, unlatched a door and let hidden things come out. Or perhaps it had been the girl, his struggle with the girl. She had got inside and bossed him, and that had set something free so he could fight back, and now there was a huge new place to explore. He must hang on to these two until he knew more about it. He was weaker than the woman but as strong as the girl. He wanted to be stronger than them both. Then he would know how to save his father. And he would know what the Dweller woman wanted him for. He did not think she meant to harm him, but she probably thought she had captured him. She was wrong. He had captured her.

He gave a little snigger and Pearl said, 'What's amusing you?'

'The way you walk. You're like a Company clerk with piles.'

'I've got sore feet,' Pearl said.

'Maybe you'd like it if I carried you?'

She turned and faced him angrily. Her face was lit by the moon, and he stepped back as she slapped at him, not with her hand but with her mind. He half parried the blow. His head rang.

'I've seen you,' he said – a face gleaming in the light of candles. 'Eating with – what is it? – forks and spoons. Men with cut-out tongues putting meat on your plate.'

'Where?' Pearl said.

'In a tree, outside your house. Was that the one I killed sitting next to you?'

'You watched us? You spied on us?'

'Not just you. All the houses. I could have sneaked inside and killed you all.'

'You talk too much about killing,' Tealeaf said.

'I had to eat the scraps out of your rubbish tins. But I pissed in your fountains.'

'Be quiet, boy,' Tealeaf said.

Pearl was panting. 'There are no men with cut-out tongues,' she whispered.

Hari shook himself. Where had his burst of hatred come from? It had rolled over him, and rolled him over, but suddenly he stood free of it. He looked at Tealeaf: had she gone inside his mind and freed him.

No, her voice said in his head, you're in charge of yourself. I don't want to look inside until you've got all your hatred out.

'That will be never,' Hari said aloud.

'Then I'm sorry for you,' Tealeaf said.

'Yes,' Hari said. 'But I never wanted to be in their house, sitting at their table. I'd rather be hunting king rats.'

'I don't sit at their table any more,' Pearl said. 'It's me my brother was hunting, to take me back and turn me into a slave.'

Hari supposed it was true. He didn't know how to answer and didn't want to argue any more. He had said he would

80

never be rid of his hatred, and the Dweller woman had said she was sorry for him. He wanted to think about that.

'I'm thirsty,' he said.

'Then let's find water.'

They walked again. After a time Hari moved closer to Pearl: 'The earth's soft here. If you take your shoes off, your feet will feel better.'

'No,' Pearl said.

'Try it, Pearl,' Tealeaf said. 'We need to go faster.'

The girl sat down and untied her boots. Hari could not believe how small and white her feet were. They reminded him of the grubs they'd eaten. But she walked more easily after that, and more easily still when the soil turned sandy.

They left the scattered ironwood trees behind, and after a while Tealeaf said, 'See that rock ahead?'

'It's not a rock,' Hari said.

'You've got good eyes. No, it's a plant.' She stopped beside it: a gnarled hump as tall as a horse, spreading out like dried mud where it touched the ground. Tiny leaves like rat ears lay on its surface. Tealeaf crouched and scratched a hole near the base.

'Dig with your knife, Hari. Pearl, use your knife. When you find a root, scrape down a little way. You'll find a sac at the end.'

Hari dug. He found a root thinner than his finger, followed it through dry sand and uncovered a tough-skinned pouch as big as his fist.

'Cut the root, hold it shut. The sac is full of water. Now squeeze it into your mouth. You too, Pearl. Have you got one?'

'It's sour,' Pearl said.

'My people call this the bounty plant.'

'Sour bounty,' Pearl said.

Hari liked the taste. It was better water than he was used to.

'Put some on your feet, Pearl. It'll help your blisters,' Tealeaf said.

They collected half a dozen sacs each, and sealed them by tying the roots.

'That's enough. Any more and the plant will die.'

They went on, walking more easily. The mountains shone with pale light. Fingers of scrubby bush reached out from the jumbled hills at their base. Hari understood how lucky he was to have met the Dweller woman. She knew the dry lands and probably knew paths through the mountains as well. Without her he might never find a way, just as he would never have found water. As for the other things she knew, he would find them out – find out how to speak and command. Then he would have a better weapon than his knife. And find out where his dreams had come from: who had sent them, what they meant. They had made him grow older in a single day.

The ground rose more steeply and turned stony. Pearl sat down and put her boots on. They shared a sac of water and plodded on towards the mountains.

FIVE

Sleep, Pearl thought, please let me sleep.

The afternoon sun burned through the spindly leaves, and the ground under her back grew a new hump every time she shifted. She tried scraping a hollow but found only more rocks. She covered her eyes with her kerchief but the light burned through.

Tealeaf slept. Hari slept. They had no trouble. Pearl turned on her side, which brought her almost face to face with the boy. How ugly he was, with his black skin and scarred face and matted hair. One of his hands lay splayed at his side. It was scarred too, probably with bites from the animals he killed or from fighting. Was that the hand that had thrown the knife? She could not believe she was lying only an arm's length away from the person who had killed her brother. He was like an animal himself, quick and savage; yet he could do what she could, use his mind in ways other people could not – except Tealeaf. She did not want to be like him. If she had to share, she wanted it to be with someone white skinned, and if it was a boy, one who was tall and handsome as well. Yet Tealeaf was not white but the colour of weak tea; and

Tealeaf, especially, was not like her – or like Hari either.

So, Pearl wondered, who are we?

She sat up quietly, and the dog raised its head and looked at her.

Who are we, dog?

It rested its chin on the ground and wagged its tail.

Pearl stood up and walked to the edge of the clearing. The scrub was over head-height and she felt enclosed. She saw rocks ahead, rising like chimneys, and thought if she could climb partway up she might see the mountains. Just the sight of snow would cool her and maybe allow her to sleep.

Come on, dog, she said, and the animal, after a nervous look at Hari, followed her.

The rock chimneys rose in front of her. They were less smooth than they had appeared from a distance, and she found handholds in the tallest and climbed above the scrub by a metre or two. There were the mountains, close enough it seemed to touch, their snowfields and ice walls gleaming in the sun. At once she felt cooler and at peace. Another night and they would be in the foothills, and reach the mountains and the snow soon after that. Tongues of bush pushed into the plain, the nearest one across a gully edging the scrub patch where they were camped. Perhaps there was a stream there. She longed for flowing water to wash in.

She climbed higher. She would ask Tealeaf if they could go into the bush and travel there instead of in the scrub, which stabbed her hands and face with its spiny leaves. She looked back the way they had travelled. The city was gone, the sea was gone, and only a brown smudge on the land's horizon showed where the smoke of the factories poured out. Bowles factories, some of them, Ottmar factories. She had never seen one. Women and girls were not supposed to know about such things.

The rock curved back, making a natural seat. She turned awkwardly and sat down, holding on to protuberances in case she slipped. The dog whined.

'I'm all right, dog,' she said. 'Lie down and rest.'

'I'm the one who tells him what to do,' Hari said. He stepped out of the scrub and frowned up at her. 'If you fall off and break your fat legs, I'm not carrying you.' He looked for a way to climb, but the only handholds were the ones she had used.

'Why should I fall?' she said. But she did not want to quarrel with Hari, she wanted to find out more about him. Some questions she could not ask – had he ever washed in his life? She could smell him from up here. But, how had he got his scars? That should be all right.

Hari, too, was curious about Pearl. He wanted to ask what some of the things tasted like that he had seen her eating at the table in her house – things that steamed, things of every colour – but just remembering them made his hatred boil up again. The dog jumped sideways and cowered.

'I'm not to blame,' Pearl said. 'What made those scars on your face?'

'The sickness,' he said.

'What sickness?'

'The one that killed my mother.' At once he was angry he had said that. It was none of her business – and it sounded as if he was asking her to be sorry for him. 'Half the people in the burrows died. How many died where you were?'

'I haven't heard of it,' Pearl said.

'Too busy eating,' he said.

'No,' she said. 'But Tealeaf has told me about the burrows.'

'How does she know?'

'Tealeaf knows everything.'

'Who is she? She's a Dweller. But what does she want?'

Yes, Pearl thought, what does Tealeaf want? Us, she thought, me and this boy.

'Why?' he said, and Pearl realised he had picked up her thought. She went on without speaking:

Because we can do what she does. We can hear what people think, and talk to each other without saying it aloud.

I'm best with animals, he said.

I haven't seen many animals. But – we can make people do things. And forget things. At least I can, I think. Can you?

'If you can, I can,' he said.

'Tealeaf will teach you. She'll teach us.'

'Why?' he said.

Because, Pearl thought, she wants us to do something. First she wanted me, and she got me. Now she's got Hari. Two of us.

She hasn't got me, Hari said. How long have you known her?

Since I was eight. I had to choose a maid – my personal maid – and I chose her. But only because she told me to.

Then she felt guilty, as if she had betrayed Tealeaf.

'She's my friend,' she said.

'She's your maid. Wipes your bum, I bet.'

'She's taught me everything I know,' Pearl said angrily.

'How to paint your face. How to comb your hair.'

'How to wash, at least. So I don't stink.'

He hissed angrily, then controlled himself. 'Lo taught me. I'd sooner have him than a Dweller. He told me how Company came and murdered my people. And starved the rest of us and made us slaves. Do you know all that?'

'I know – I know that Company is everywhere. And cares for nothing but itself. And makes me a slave too – makes me marry who it wants.'

'You're a slave with plenty to eat,' Hari said. 'And a maid.'
He turned away. 'Come on, dog, let's leave her sitting on her
throne.'

'Wait,' Pearl said. Then urgently: Wait. Come back.

What? he said.

Something out there, moving, in the hills.

Let me see.

She stood up on the rock seat, peering out, and Hari climbed
until his head was level with her knees. She pointed.

Men on horses, she said.

Following dogs. It's Company.

Tealeaf, Pearl shouted soundlessly.

They climbed down from the rock and ran through the
scrub, where they met Tealeaf hurrying towards them.

My father's men are coming. The dogs have got our scent.

'How far away?'

'Half an hour. Maybe less,' Hari said.

'There's a gully,' Pearl said, pointing. 'And bush on the
other side. We can hide there.'

They ran to their sleeping place and snatched up their
packs.

'Run, Pearl. I'll follow,' Tealeaf said.

'What are you doing?'

'Go. Fast.'

Pearl and Hari ran.

'Can you hear her?' Hari said. 'She's leaving fangcat
thoughts for the dogs. They'll pick them up. They'll run all
the way home.' He laughed, and the dog howled.

'Shut up, dog. You're safe.'

They left the scrub and started into the gully, moving fast
down the shallow slope. In a few moments Tealeaf overtook
them.

'They're close. I heard them at the edge of the scrub.'

'They must want to grab you badly,' Hari said. 'Getting here so quick.'

'Maybe it's you they want for killing my brother,' Pearl said.

'Don't talk, just run,' Tealeaf said.

In a moment they heard the shrieking of dogs. A quick command from Tealeaf kept their dog from joining in.

'Will the horses bolt?'

'The riders will control them. But they won't be able to make them follow in the scrub. No more talk. Fast.'

The gully was wider than Pearl had thought. They reached the bottom and began climbing towards the bush. A thin shout came coiling down at them.

'It's someone on the rock I climbed,' Pearl cried.

They saw the man pointing, saw him leap down.

Faster, Tealeaf ordered. As fast as you can.

Their feet slid on loose stones. Behind them men on foot burst from the scrub and ran down the slope. A dozen on horses came round the bottom edge. One stopped to fire shots from his bolt gun, but the distance was too great.

'Alive,' someone shouted. 'I want them alive.'

The horses galloped along the gully bed and their riders began to force them up the slope. Hari turned, but there were too many for him to command – and too many for Tealeaf, he supposed. He ran beside the women, sliding and stumbling like them, but saw that they would reach the bush before the riders overtook them.

Whoever commanded the horsemen saw it too. He called them back and assembled them in the gully.

Tealeaf, Pearl and Hari ran into the trees where the trunks sheltered them. They paused for breath.

'What are they doing?' Pearl said.

'Whoever it is, he's clever,' Tealeaf said.

The man in charge was young. Pearl recognised his Ottmar red and green cloak. The lances of his horsemen were adorned with the Ottmar pennant.

'It's one of Ottmar's sons, so it's me they want,' Pearl said.

'Ottmar owns the salt mines,' Hari said. He drew his knife.

'Put it away,' Tealeaf said. 'We'll see what he does.'

The men on foot started back round the scrub for their horses. Two bands of horsemen broke away, each five strong. One headed towards the place where the tongue of bush poked from thicker bush. The other rode fast the opposite way, round the tip of the tongue.

'They're surrounding us,' Hari said.

'What they'll do,' Tealeaf said, 'is burn a barrier with their guns so we can't get into the hills. Then they'll hunt us out into the open.'

'How many are there? I can kill them,' Hari said.

'Fifty. A squadron,' Pearl said.

In a moment they heard bolt guns firing, and soon a column of smoke rose into the sky.

'They've cut us off,' Tealeaf said calmly. 'Now they'll come down through the bush. See, more men are going. But it will be night before they find us.'

'There'll be a full moon,' Pearl said.

'Yes. We'll only have darkness for an hour. Well, we'll see. I must watch this clever young man. He's not in any hurry.'

'He's coming up.'

The man spurred his horse up the slope, but stopped halfway to the bush.

'Radiant Pearl of the Deep Blue Sea,' he shouted.

'Don't answer,' Tealeaf said.

'Can you hear me, Pearl?'

'It's the youngest son. I danced with him at the ball,' Pearl said.

'Radiant Pearl. My name is Kyle-Ott of Ottmar's house. My father has sent me to collect his bride. He keeps a place for you in his kitchen.'

The men in the gully jeered and laughed.

'You're running with vermin, Pearl. You hide in ditches when you might have sat at his side. You have made your choice. I will carry you back tied across my saddle, the way your brother Hubert was tied. And the Dweller woman. But I will cut the heart out of the burrows rat running with you. As a gift, Pearl, to avenge your brother.'

'He hides something,' Tealeaf whispered, 'but he's too far away for me to read it.'

Pearl, hidden deep in ferns, stared at the young man's face – his smiling mouth, his hawk nose, his blue icy eyes. It was Ottmar's face without its pouches, without its fat. She had once thought Kyle-Ott was handsome.

'By nightfall, Pearl, I will have you scuttling out of there. Meanwhile, think of your fate.'

He turned his horse and rode back to the gully bed.

'All right,' Tealeaf said. 'Now we move ahead of these men coming through the bush. I don't want them catching us before the sun goes down.'

They went deeper into the bush, then Tealeaf fell behind and spoke to Hari: They mustn't catch you. But I think you have skills to hide yourself. Wait until it's nearly dark, then find a place.

I'll come back, he said.

I know you will.

They kept moving towards the tip of the bush. The afternoon wore on, the sun dipped in the sky as the cries of the men sweeping the bush came closer.

Now, Hari, Tealeaf said, and he gave a nod.

Stay with them, dog, he said, and slipped away.

He already had his hiding place worked out, a forest of low ferns between tree trunks, and he ran back to it quickly, hearing the calls of the men and the crackle of undergrowth as they approached. He fastened his bag tightly on his back, then lay down and wriggled like a snake into the ferns, turning and twisting, leaving no snapped twig or bent leaf. Tough fronds covered him like a cloak. He stilled his breathing, then drew his knife, just in case.

The men were too far apart to make a close search. They kept their bolt guns glowing for light in the gloom of the bush and shouted to each other, back and forth, driving prey rather than searching. The one who passed the fern patch gave it no glance. His boots crushed stems on its outer edge; he kicked a rotten branch out of his way and went on.

Hari waited until the sounds were gone. Then he rose from the ferns and ran through the bush. There was still no way out. Horsemen would be waiting around the edges and others at the fire that still burned. But he had no thought of escape. He meant to stay close to the Dweller woman and use her to find his father. So he must watch what happened and work out what to do. She seemed unconcerned at being captured, but did not seem to have a plan for getting away.

He sat beside a tree and ate a handful of roasted grubs and drank a sac of water. Then he chose a tall tree and climbed the creepers strangling its trunk. He went up through branches until he could see over the heads of smaller trees. The sun was low. He shaded his eyes. The troop of horsemen waited where the gully met the plain. He could not see the searchers in the bush, but they must be close to the bottom edge – close to forcing Tealeaf and Pearl into the open.

Hari watched, making no plan. First he needed to see where everyone was, then he would know what to do.

He heard, distantly, a shouted command: Kyle-Ott. The

horsemen fanned out. But there was no need for them to chase, as Tealeaf and Pearl walked from the bush. Hari saw them move towards the setting sun, saw horses surround them and Kyle-Ott dismount. Tealeaf seemed unconcerned, even when Kyle-Ott forced her to kneel. What was he doing? Tying something around her eyes? He must know, somehow, that she had powers to control other people, and think it came from her cat eyes. He did not blindfold Pearl, although his men kept her and Tealeaf covered with their bolt guns.

Hari climbed down and used the last few minutes of light to work his way through the bush. As darkness fell, sudden, complete, he reached the edge above the gully.

Kyle-Ott's men had gathered scrub to make a fire, and they sat about it eating a meal. Kyle-Ott sat by a smaller fire, with Tealeaf, blindfolded, and Pearl sitting with him. Tealeaf had her arms tied. Pearl was free.

Further up the gully, Hari made out the sound of horses. They must be tethered there, with someone guarding them. One man? Two? He would have to wait until the moon came up.

And by that time he needed to be much closer than this.

He called silently for the dog.

Kyle-Ott's teeth gleamed in the firelight. 'It gives me no pleasure to see you broken, Pearl. There was a time when I thought you might serve as a bride for me. Radiant Pearl is a name that suits you. But alas, my father had first choice.' He leaned forward and smiled. 'At least you did not dishonour me. I warn you, he is angry, my father. It will not be a pleasant time for you.'

'I'm not afraid,' Pearl said, although she was.

Kyle-Ott – seventeen summers, he was not much older than Hari – stirred the fire with a stick.

'He gave me this task, to bring you back, and I will complete it. I am the youngest son, Pearl. Chasing a runaway bride is fit for me. So my brothers think. While they –' he made a savage lunge with the stick, scattering flame – 'they concern themselves with greater things. But they are fools, Pearl. He uses them as weapons, to stab and slash, and keeps me hidden away.' His voice sank to a whisper. 'I am his favourite. When I return to the city . . .' He completed the sentence with a smile.

Tealeaf's voice sounded in Pearl's head: Ask him what is happening in the city.

Why? What does it matter? Pearl said.

He keeps it hidden. I need to know. His vanity will make him talk. Be afraid, if you can. Flatter him.

Pearl grimaced inwardly. She set herself. 'Isn't there some way . . .?' she faltered.

'What, Pearl?' he said softly. 'To save you from the fate you have deserved? You're a pretty thing and would look . . .' he sought for words '. . . charming at my side. But there will be plenty more – and you belong to my father.' He made a false shrug. 'It is sad.'

'But your father is only one man, and if you petition Company . . .?'

'Ah, Pearl,' he smiled, 'you haven't heard. There are changes, great changes in the city. Even as we sit here it is done, this very night.' His face suddenly grew ugly. 'And I'm chasing a stupid girl. I'd rather run my hounds at you like some burrows rat.' He brooded. 'The world is overturned, and I sit here.'

'But your father . . .' Pearl whispered.

'My father keeps me safe. I'm his right hand. Or soon will be, when I bring you back. Did you know –' he hesitated, then made a decision and grinned at her – 'Company has fallen?

93

My father was the one who saw it coming; he read the signs, while all the other fools, Bowles and Kruger and Sinclair, all of them, sat blind and fat and happy, and spent their money on their pretty daughters and couldn't see what was under their noses. But my father – he has spies and informers everywhere, even over the sea. There have been no ships for many months, did you know that, Pearl? Your father saw, but he took no notice. No trade. No message. Only Ottmar understood. He learned the reason long before the others. The rabble rose up in those great lands. They overthrew Company, and now a thousand petty rulers sit on thrones and fight each other. Darkness there, Pearl. Darkness. My father saw it creep on the horizon. It will last for a thousand years. He alone saw. And he was ready. There is no Company in our land any more. There is a king. A great king.'

'Who . . .?' Pearl managed to say.

'King Ottmar. And when my brothers are gone – and he will see to that – I will be his heir. Kyle-Ott.'

'But my father? My family? My brothers?'

'He may find a use for them – although House Bowles is out of favour, Pearl, thanks to you. But who knows? If not – there's an old tradition of throwing traitors from the cliffs.'

'You're lying. You're making it up.'

No, Pearl, Tealeaf said, he's telling the truth. There haven't been any ships, and now we know the reason. Ottmar seized his chance. Ask this foolish boy what the new king will do.

Pearl swallowed. She thought of her proud father and mother locked in dungeons. She thought of her sister, Blossom, and her brothers, William and George. They would not bow down: stupid, spoiled, greedy, they would fight. But mostly she thought of the woman, Tilly, who had sheltered her and Tealeaf. What would happen to Tilly and her husband and baby? With Ottmar as king, they would be slaves. Kyle-Ott moved on with his boasting but Pearl scarcely listened.

Tealeaf said, 'What will King Ottmar do in the city, in his lands?'

'Ah, the Dweller has a voice. But no eyes, Dweller. My father learned the secret of that. You can make men sleep, and make them do things against their will. He asked me to bring you back so he can find out why. My father will be a great king.'

'What will he do in his lands?' Tealeaf repeated evenly.

'He will rule.' Kyle-Ott closed his fist. 'Like that. There is room only for one voice. One man. He will cleanse the land. He will scour the burrows, wipe out the vermin there, build Ottmar, a city worthy of our family name, where he and I can rule and no other voice be heard. That is the way. With strength. Without pity. Does it please you, Dweller?'

'I believe you'll try,' Tealeaf said. 'What of my people?'

'Ah yes, beyond the mountains, in the forests, where you live like swamp-rats. We have heard of you. Company hasn't found a use for Dwellers. But Ottmar and Kyle-Ott will come. Our armies will come. You will bow down. Meanwhile, when I take you back, we will break you open and learn your secrets.'

He called a man from beyond the firelight. 'Tie her blindfold tighter. Bind her arms tighter. And tie the girl now. Watch them all night. Don't let them speak.'

'We haven't found the boy, Lord,' the man said.

'No matter. He has burrowed in some hole. Let him starve.'

Two men raised a small tent, emblazoned with the Ottmar coat of arms. Others bound Tealeaf tighter and tied Pearl's hands and feet. They pushed them down on the ground and threw a covering over them – 'I don't want you frozen,' Kyle-Ott said. 'My father asks for you in good condition. But consider, Pearl, this bed of stones is more comfortable than any you will know for the rest of your life.' He turned to his sergeant – 'Guard them' – and retired to his tent.

Pearl and Tealeaf lay side by side. The moon came up and sat in the bowl of hills like an orange, then climbed lazily into the sky.

Is it true? Pearl asked. Everything he says?

What is happening now, back in the city, yes, it's true. And over the sea. True, I suppose. But what he says about the future – we'll see.

King Ottmar?

Yes, King Ottmar.

He'll be worse than Company.

He'll be different. Now wait a while, Pearl. Sleep if you can. Don't watch for Hari. He'll choose his time.

What will he do?

I don't know. But I can feel him close. We'll wait and see. Sleep now.

She said it the way she had when Pearl was a child, when it had drifted her away dreamlessly, but Pearl resisted now. She tried to feel Hari. If he came to rescue them she meant to be awake, not lying like a parcel to be untied. The man who had bound her had been nervous – she was, after all, the daughter of a great house, Bowles – and she had gasped and shrunk as though he hurt her, so the cords were not as tight as he might have made them.

Pearl turned and sighed and pretended to sleep, with her back to the fire. The watchmen yawned and dozed, but one always seemed to be awake. Why couldn't Tealeaf put him to sleep? And Pearl could do it herself, if she tried. She was sure of it. Instead she worked with slow movements, pulling one wrist back against the other, then reversing it.

You'll only tighten the knots, Pearl, Tealeaf said.

No, I won't. If I can use my teeth . . .

She rolled again and used the movement to bring her wrists up to her face.

'Sleep, girl,' growled a guard.

'I'm trying,' she said.

She worked with her teeth, covering the bites with little sobs, as though she was crying and wiping her eyes.

Tealeaf, I've done it. My hands are free.

Don't try your feet. He'll see that.

Where's Hari?

At the horses.

Are you talking to him?

Listen and you'll hear. Forget your knots.

Hari, she whispered.

From far away his voice came back: Keep quiet, you.

Hari, we left the dog in the bush.

I called him. He's here.

Pearl sighed, then felt a sharp pain, a stabbing like a needle, behind her eyes.

Tealeaf, what happened?

Nothing.

I felt it. Tealeaf – has he . . .?

He had to throw his knife, Pearl. The man guarding the horses saw him.

He could have put him to sleep.

He wasn't sure he could do it. And he didn't have time.

No time, Hari's voice echoed. I tried not to . . .

Hari, Tealeaf said, be still a moment.

I couldn't . . . there was nothing . . .

Be still.

A moment passed – no voices, no sound but ash falling in the fire.

Is he all right? Pearl said.

It goes against a dream he had. He doesn't want to kill.

They lay still, waiting, and in a moment Hari's voice spoke again: The horses are afraid of me. The man was their friend. I'm trying to make them calm.

Beyond the large fire, where the men of the squadron lay sleeping, a horse whinnied. The guards at the smaller fire woke from their doze.

'Fangcat?' one of them whispered.

'They'd be bolting if it was,' the sergeant said. 'More likely a dog.'

They listened, and two or three more whinnies came through the moonlight, followed by a trampling of hooves.

'Something's spooking them. You two go and see,' the sergeant said.

'What if it's a cat?'

'Use your guns.'

Hari, Pearl said, two men are coming.

I can't make the horses trust me. I'll have to stampede them, he replied.

Drive them through the camp. Use the dog, Tealeaf said.

I'm cutting their tethers. Get behind the fire. I'm thinking fangcat.

Terrified whinnies and shrieks rang out. Hoofs thundered. The men by the large fire jumped to their feet. The sound of hooves increased, like a storm rolling out of the sky. The guards by the small fire ran to the larger one. Kyle-Ott scrambled from his tent, struggling into his shirt.

'What's happening?' he shrieked, his voice breaking into a falsetto. He ran after the guards – and the horses burst like a black wave over the crest of the moonlit slope and ran at the fire.

Pearl worked at her bound feet, while Tealeaf rolled into the protection of the fire. Pearl freed her feet, ran to her and plucked off her blindfold. She started on her hands, then saw that Tealeaf had almost freed herself.

The horses broke on either side of the large fire, scattering men, bowling them like dummies. Kyle-Ott, his hands held high, shouted commands, and some of the men tried to clutch the horses' manes as they thundered by. Kyle-Ott tried, but the horse he ran at sent him reeling backwards, and another knocked him sideways into the fire, where he scrambled, howling, through the embers.

The leading horses reached the smaller fire and broke around it. They trampled Kyle-Ott's tent into the ground. Pearl and Tealeaf huddled close to the dying flames, but one horse, finding no path, leaped across, and his flying hoof struck Tealeaf on the forehead. She fell in a heap.

'Tealeaf,' Pearl cried, but the Dweller made no sound.

The horses were gone, rolling away like a dying storm.

'Chase them. Find them,' Kyle-Ott cried. He ran after his men a few steps, then turned back; he advanced on Pearl, with smoking clothes and maniacal face.

'She did this. The Dweller.'

In a frenzy he searched in his trampled tent, found his stabbing sword, tore it from its scabbard and ran at Tealeaf. Pearl rose to face him. She glimpsed Hari and the dog running by the scattered embers of the larger fire. Hari had his knife out, ready to throw,

'No,' Pearl cried, and cried again: No.

Hari lowered the knife.

Kyle-Ott was three steps from Tealeaf, his sword raised two-handed. Pearl stepped over her friend, sheltering her. She looked into Kyle-Ott's burned face, into his eyes.

Stop there, she ordered him. Be still.

He reeled as though he had run into a wall. He stood swaying, with his mouth wide and eyes unfocused.

Put down your sword.

He obeyed.

Gather your men. Find your horses. Go back to your city. Do it now.

He turned away.

Kyle-Ott, Pearl said.

He turned back.

Tell your father he will never be king.

She did not know where those words came from, but repeated: Never. Tell him that. Now go.

Kyle-Ott stumbled away.

Hari advanced to the fire. 'You should have made him walk all the way.'

'Help me with Tealeaf.'

The Dweller woman opened her eyes. For a moment her cat pupils were almost round, then they narrowed to their usual shape. Pearl searched for her pack, found a water sac and helped Tealeaf drink. She told her what had happened, what she had done with Kyle-Ott.

'They'll come back for their gear, though, and their wounded.' Hari indicated half a dozen trampled men. 'So let's get out of here.'

They took nothing but their packs from Kyle-Ott's camp. With Pearl and Hari helping Tealeaf by turns, they went along the gully and climbed towards the foothills. The moon crossed the sky and dropped below the horizon. The sun came up and poured its light down the mountain slopes.

They entered the bush, found a dry safe place, ate the last of the grubs, drank the last water, and slept.

SIX

The mountains were dark and cold, and the passes high and the paths that climbed to them precipitous. On the warmer northern side the bush thickened to jungle. It oppressed Pearl. She had been happier in the clear air, even when the wind blew ice crystals in her face. It had taken six days of climbing to the final pass, broken by cold uncomfortable nights. Hari revelled in the hardship, while she gritted her teeth and plodded on. Sometimes she picked up the dog and carried him for an hour, holding him to share their warmth. The dog suffered, his feet grew raw, and Tealeaf made cloth boots for him, cut off her cloak. Cold, hungry, were his only thoughts, and Pearl, conversing with him, made images of hearths and fires and meat. She wanted meat for herself. The food Tealeaf had gathered in the bush on the southern hills – fruit, grubs, roots, edible leaves – was nourishing, she felt it in her blood, felt it strengthening her, but so much chewing was called for and so many bitter tastes had to be endured.

Hari ate without complaint. Food was something that had to be fought for, and grabbed at, and eaten fast. It was a luxury for him to be able to dip into the bag at his side, squeeze the poison out of a grub, bite off and spit out its head, and swallow it whole. When they reached the snow he killed a snow hare and they roasted it on a fire of ironwood twigs Tealeaf had made him carry for that purpose. It was their only meat, but they were in the snow for only two days and a night.

Their first view north of the mountains showed bare scree slopes, then dry hills, followed by jungles stretching away. Lakes shone like windows, while here and there loops of river curved as white as knife blades in the trees.

'Where's Deep Salt?' Hari asked.

'Do you see where the mountains turn westwards?' Tealeaf said.

'That far?'

'The salt mines are at the seaward end, south from where I'm taking you. And Deep Salt –' she grimaced – 'lies deeper.'

'So we've got to cross the jungle?' Hari said.

'There are ways,' Tealeaf said. 'But first, let's get down out of this cold.'

Two more days brought them into hills, and another two into the jungle. Food became more plentiful and varied. They took fish from the rivers, nuts from the trees and seeds from the plants. Tealeaf mesmerised wild bees with a low monotonous humming while Pearl and Hari stole honey. They followed a river that tumbled through rapids then ran slow and lazy through trees whose plate-sized leaves dipped into the water. Biting flies attacked them, and Tealeaf made a toadstool paste and smeared it on their faces and arms to keep them off.

Soon the understorey grew more dense.

'We're being watched. Do you feel it?' Tealeaf said.

'It's like someone brushing inside my head. Or brushing my hair the wrong way,' Pearl said.

'Are they dangerous?' Hari said.

'Not if we only take what we need. I spoke with them on the edge of the jungle while you were sleeping.'

'Who are they? What do they look like?'

'I said I spoke. I didn't say I saw.'

'We could send the dog to find them,' Pearl said.

'The dog would never come back. No one sees. They haven't got a name, so we give them none. The jungle is theirs and always will be.'

'It's like being in the burrows. They could kill us,' Hari said. He felt both helpless and aggressive.

'They wouldn't need to. They'd let the jungle do it. But Dwellers have never hurt them, so they let us pass.'

'I wouldn't have got through on my own,' Hari said.

He crouched closer to the fire and threw another branch on. The new flames made Tealeaf's face shine red. She had begun to seem stranger since they had entered the jungle: her three-fingered hands, performing their tasks, were more dextrous – they moved so fast Hari thought of the shimmering wings of the bees whose honey they had robbed – and her eyes had turned a jungle green. She talked less with her tongue and more with a 'voice' that penetrated Hari like a thin silver-bladed knife. He wondered if she was letting him know that, in a way, he belonged to her. She was wrong about that, and he would show her when the time was right.

'There are creatures that hunt in the night. And the daytime too. So don't even think about running away,' Tealeaf said.

'Why don't they come, then? We're an easy feed sitting here.'

If you stop speaking with your tongue and use your 'voice' you'll hear why not. The jungle isn't silent, it never is. Hear the hunting cries, far away?

Hari listened; and heard, far off, the scream of an animal dying. Closer, something roared with rage at not making the kill itself.

It's a savage place, Tealeaf said.

'Why don't they come for us?' Pearl whispered.

Hush, Pearl. Listen. Listen, Hari.

The jungle continued its night-bird cries and tree-animal whoopings, but underneath these sounds a softer, more delicate one, monotonous, almost unheard, slowly established itself.

Do you hear? Tealeaf said. It began when we entered the jungle and won't stop till we leave.

What is it? they whispered.

The people with no name. They've woven a circle around us to keep us safe. They know the pitch of sound that keeps each animal away. They're protecting us.

Why?

It's part of their pact with Dwellers. I asked if we could travel through, and they agreed.

Sshh, Pearl said. She listened to the soft bee-note surrounding them. It's like music.

The tree tiger doesn't think so. Nor does the night bear.

Nor does the dog. That's why you tied that cloth around his head, Hari said.

Yes, the dog's unhappy. But it won't last.

'You've got too many secrets,' Hari said. 'I'm going to sleep. Wake me if these people we can't see stop singing. I've still got my knife.'

He pulled the dog close to him and lay down by the fire.

Pearl moved closer to Tealeaf. She longed for the times when Tealeaf had brushed and plaited her hair and helped her dress – and when, in private, they had sat down and talked, talked aloud and then in silence, and been no longer

104

mistress and servant but two people sharing equally. She missed the lessons, the thrill of learning things no one else in the city knew. Now Tealeaf seemed to be moving away – although she had told them about the people with no name. But that had been to stop Hari behaving stupidly.

Tealeaf's voice came whispering silently into her mind: Trust me, Pearl.

Are we still friends?

More than ever. More than you can know.

It's like he says: you've got too many secrets.

Soon, Pearl, as soon as we're out of the jungle and you've met my people . . .

Met other Dwellers?

Yes. When we come out of these black trees into the green . . .

Do you live there?

I used to, in a village called Stone Creek. I've got so much to think about, Pearl, that's why I've gone away from you. And I've got to watch Hari or he'll do something stupid. She smiled and touched Pearl's hand. Go to sleep now. Tomorrow's hard work. We travel on the river.

I like hard work. It's better than eiderdowns and perfumes and sweetmeats.

Tealeaf laughed, a clear sound competing with the cruel noises of the jungle. She touched Pearl's hand again.

'Go to sleep.'

The spoken words were more comforting than silent ones. Pearl wrapped herself in her cloak and lay down by the fire, opposite Hari. His unwashed smell still troubled her, but she supposed she was starting to smell the same herself. It made her frown, then almost laugh. She went to sleep.

Tealeaf put more wood on the fire, then slept a while herself, sitting up; and woke and fed the fire again, and waited; and after an hour, in the darkest time of the night, her face altered, grew entranced as something, some thing, with a silent voice, spoke to her. If Pearl had woken then she would not have known Tealeaf – but Pearl did not wake. She was having her own dream. It was not of people or animals or places, and there was neither then or now. It took her deep into itself, while speaking no word but her name. It told her its own name, which Pearl did not understand, except that somehow it meant all things, everywhere, and it told her, without saying, that a door was open and she could enter when she chose.

She did not wake at the end of the dream. She slept more deeply. She did not remember it or forget. It stayed inside her. When she woke in the morning she was different but did not know why, or why the first thought she had was: I am Pearl.

Tealeaf was different too; was strengthened and less brooding, as though she had shaken off a sickness. She moved more lightly and her face, always fine boned and hollow cheeked, seemed more full. Yet when she noticed Pearl staring into the jungle she grew still, and took a step away as if to study her, and after a moment she made a dipping motion with her head, and a sigh of contentment, and said to Pearl: Did you sleep well?

When Pearl replied: I had dreams but I can't remember what they were, she laughed and said: 'Eat some grubs, then. We'd better get started.' But she hummed a tune Pearl had never heard before as she prepared the food.

Hari, meanwhile, was ready to go. He thought of little but Deep Salt and his father. The sounds of the people with no name, present intermittently in the jungle, made him frown. He was used to fighting his own battles and did not like depending on other people, especially when he couldn't see them.

They travelled through the understorey, breaking their way, and came to a river at mid-morning. A dugout canoe, shallow and broad, was waiting on a stony beach. They paddled for the rest of the day, slept on the bank at night – eating fish, boiling river water – and went on the next morning until falls forced them to leave the canoe.

Back deep in the jungle at night, they crouched around their fire and listened to the noises of hunting animals and the encircling humming that kept them safe. Hari remembered how, looking from the mountains, he had seen the jungle stretching to another range in the north, but going on and on in the east in a widening valley until it was lost in a haze. And Tealeaf had said that it stretched beyond that as if forever. It made him shiver and long for the world he knew, of ruined buildings and tottering walls, where the most dangerous thing was a king rat or a pack of starving dogs. He could hear a voice speaking in this jungle. He did not think it spoke to him. Perhaps it was the voice Lo heard when the curtain lifted. But Lo seemed far away and the jungle seemed to emphasise that he had known very little. And Hari wanted to know little himself – not what Pearl knew, with her changed face and air of waiting, or Tealeaf, who was different because she was a Dweller; he wanted only to perfect his skill in speaking and, more importantly, in controlling, so he could use them to find his father. The only other thing he needed to know was the meaning of his dream – that dream of violence and peace. What had it instructed him to do as he lay asleep after his first encounter with Pearl? And how did it help in his search for his father?

SEVEN

Tealeaf's village, Stone Creek, disappointed Pearl. She had expected buildings with fantastic shapes, but everything was simple and unadorned. Small houses with timber walls lined the streets. Beyond them the sea gleamed. Half a dozen wooden boats, big enough for two or three people, were drawn up on a white-sand beach between low headlands. Their shipped oars poked out like insect legs.

'It's tiny,' she complained.

'It's as big as it needs to be,' Tealeaf answered.

'You could fit this place in People's Square,' Hari said. But he had little interest. He wanted to eat, and then he wanted to know where Deep Salt was. 'Do they know we're coming?'

'We're expected. We'll go to my brother's house. Tomorrow you can meet our council and ask your questions. You too, Pearl. All your questions.'

'Do we speak out loud?'

'Whatever you're comfortable with.'

They walked along cobbled streets until they reached a footway above the foreshore. Tealeaf turned past houses facing the sea, where lamps were being lit as the sun went down. People opened doors and windows and greeted them. Tealeaf's face lit up with pleasure, and Pearl guessed that messages she could not hear must be reaching her – of welcome home, of love perhaps – and something she'd never thought of suddenly struck her.

Tealeaf, she whispered, are you married?

No, Pearl. There were other things I chose to do.

Like finding me, Pearl said, and was guilty and sad. She felt sadness in Tealeaf too, and knew there had been someone she had loved and would have married if she had not chosen another way. Or perhaps she hadn't chosen; perhaps she had been told or ordered, and had obeyed.

No, Pearl, it wasn't like that, Tealeaf said.

Was there someone?

Yes.

Where is he?

It seemed for a moment Tealeaf wouldn't answer. Then she said: He has a wife now, and children. He's happy. And I'm happy. So don't be sad for me.

You're sad for yourself.

'Oh,' Tealeaf said, 'it's natural. Now here's my brother's house, and here is Sartok, my brother.'

Tealeaf embraced the tall Dweller at the door, and Pearl heard, Hari heard too, in an almost bee-like humming in their minds – a sound like flowers, Pearl thought, a sound like honey – the depth of their brother and sister love and their delight in seeing each other again. Children crowded round Sartok's legs, and his wife, Eentel, slipped under his arm to join the embrace. The greetings took a long time. Pearl waited patiently, and Hari impatiently, while the dog, at their heels, sniffed the warm aroma-laden air coming through the door.

At length Tealeaf said: Pearl, Hari, and the two heard a

welcome, grave and formal, from Sartok and Eentel, and a chatter of interest from the children; and then they were inside a room where a table was laid and food spread out. Conversation, half spoken, half thought, eddied around them, drew them in. It was so natural and easy that they had laid down their packs and washed their hands and faces in basins of water on a side-table and dried them with cloths the children held out, and were sitting at the table eating soup and bread before they realised how much they were telling about their journey and their lives in the city. Pearl was astonished and appalled by Hari's life as he described it – the squalid hall called Dorm, the fights between scavenging bands from different burrows, the hunting of rats for food, the doling out of meagre supplies from Company carts, just enough to keep the half-starved population alive, the raids by the Whips, the shackling and branding; and Hari, although he had spied at mansion windows many times, was disbelieving at first, then simmered with anger and contempt at the luxury and waste of the life Pearl had led. It was all new to Sartok and Eentel and their children (two boys, two girls) and Pearl could see how it saddened the adults. They comforted the children with words and touches when Hari's story made them afraid.

The meal went on with a dish of meat and vegetables – the dog, by Hari's chair, got his share – followed by sweet dumplings and fruit, and mugs of tea.

You're tired, Pearl, Tealeaf said.

Yes, she replied, and felt the whole weight of her escape from her family and the city, the days, the weeks of walking, and the fear of recapture, the fear of strangeness, come down on her mind like a hand squashing an inflated bladder. She wanted to put her head on the table and sleep. Yet there was something sliding out from under the weight – something light and coloured and on the edge of sight, made of the dreams she had had on their journey and the voices she had heard in the jungle, and of a single voice, scarcely a breath, even further away, saying her name, saying: Pearl. Where was it from? What did it mean? And had she heard it or only imagined that she heard?

I'm tired, she thought. Tealeaf is right.

Hari, you need to sleep too, Tealeaf said.

'Yes, I do,' Hari said grudgingly. He had enjoyed the food, had torn at it at first and gobbled it, then seen that the others were slower and had ways that he supposed were the manners Pearl had told him he didn't have, so he slowed down and watched and learned. It wasn't important, but he needed these people – if they were people – to show him the way to Deep Salt, so for a while he would do things in their way. But Tealeaf was right: he was tired, he needed sleep, he needed to be fresh in the morning. He felt too that in describing his life in Blood Burrow he had drawn it together, held it in his hand, and that when he went back to the city he would know how to change everything. He was surprised. Am I going back? He had not known it. All he had known was that he must rescue his father. But now . . .

I'll push Company off the cliff into the sea, he thought.

Tealeaf took Pearl first, then Hari, through a back yard, where they stripped off their clothes and washed at a trough of warm water in a steam room. Hari did not know what he was meant to do. He had never washed in his life. The oldest boy, Antok, showed him how to use soap. The suds turned grey with the dirt on Hari's body, and Antok sluiced them off with buckets of water. Hari itched. The dog slunk off and hid behind the shed but came inside to sleep in the warmth when the washing was over.

They found fresh clothes laid out in their sleeping cells.

Tealeaf took away the old ones, torn and stained from the jungle, to be burned.

Pearl slept, Hari slept, both dreamless.

In the morning they ate a breakfast of grain softened in milk and cooked with dried fruit. This was followed by eggs and bread. New food for Hari. He had never seen an egg. New food for Pearl too, who had never been offered anything so simple – except muggy grubs. Well fed, comfortable in their new clothes, they walked along the foreshore with Tealeaf and Sartok until they came to a small house beside a creek emptying into the sea.

'This is where our council meets today. At other times it's in other houses. Or nowhere at all.'

'You mean you meet without talking if you want to?'

'Yes, sometimes. Other times it's good to see faces.'

'What's the council?' Hari said.

'Anyone who wants to speak or hear. I told most people about you last night, while you were sleeping. Who you are. Where you come from.'

'And where we're going? Where I'm going?' Hari said.

'Yes, Hari. Shall we go in?'

There were only three people in the house: an old man, a middle-aged woman and a boy. They welcomed Pearl and Hari formally, which set Hari on edge. Too much of this. He was used to quickness, seeing quickly, getting away fast. Pearl handled it better, saying how pleased they were to be in the village and to be made so welcome. The old man, Gantok, the woman, Teelar, listened politely, but the boy, watching Hari, seemed impatient. His name was Danatok. He sat down in a chair at a table almost filling the room and said silently: Hari, sit by me. I want to know about your father.

They took him to Deep Salt, Hari said. I'm going to get him.

112

What sort of man is he?

He's the best hunter in Blood Burrow. The best fighter. He's killed more king rats than anyone else.

King rats? They're big? As big as your dog? Danatok said.

Some are bigger. But my father kills them.

For food?

The big ones are tough. The young ones are tender. Good meat.

Is that his knife you're wearing?

Hari took it from its sheath and laid it on the table but kept his hand on it jealously.

A Dweller knife, said the old man, Gantok, peering at it. He too spoke silently. Hari, will you let me hold it for a moment?

Hari lifted his hand reluctantly and Gantok, with a small gesture of thanks, picked the knife up.

Ah, see how my hand fits. If your father learned to use this, he's kin in his heart with Dwellers.

I've learned it too, Hari said.

It is black steel, forged in the villages of the north. See the mark on the blade, two round stones rubbing together? Sunderlok's mark, the great traveller. It was made for him many years ago. He came through our village in my father's time, on his way to visit your city, Hari, and find out what was happening there. It was in the time of the man called Cowl, when he had made himself king. Sunderlok never returned. The great war started, when Company came back. Sunderlok died. Even so far away we heard the pain of his death. And this is his knife.

He laid it on the table. Yours, Hari.

My father found it in Blood Burrow, lying in the corner of a room.

Perhaps it was meant for him. I can feel from the way it

trembles that it has killed men. It was not forged for that.

You have to kill where I come from, or else you get killed. I can't feel it trembling.

Your knife, Gantok repeated. Use it as you must.

Hari sheathed the knife. These people don't know anything, he thought. But he remembered his conflicting dreams, of peace and slaughter, and grew confused. He wanted to know where he must go to find his father and what to do when he got there.

Is someone going to tell me about Deep Salt, he said.

First, Pearl said, I want to know why Tealeaf brought us here. And why she chose me. Tealeaf, you promised to tell us.

No, Hari said, Deep Salt first. Then I can go, and you can sit here listening if you want to.

You can't go yet. Not today. Not even tomorrow, the woman, Teelar, said.

Why not?

Because the one who guides you isn't ready.

I don't need a guide. Just tell me where.

Hari, Tealeaf said, don't be impatient. There's no way you can reach Deep Salt by yourself.

Why? Is it far?

Not far. Two days' travel. But – there are difficulties. And only one guide knows the way.

Who is he? The guide?

He's sitting beside you.

My son, Danatok, Teelar said. And it's too soon for him to go.

Him? Hari said with disdain. He's too small. Can he fight?

There will be no fighting.

Hari, listen, Tealeaf said. And be still. And think a while before you speak.

114

Her voice in his head pushed him back into himself, away from the dartings of his brain that carried him into fear and impatience, and contempt for these Dwellers, and into his love for his father, so that he seemed broken into pieces. He subsided.

'All right,' he said aloud.

There have only ever been two or three Dwellers able to find the way into Deep Salt and come out alive. Danatok is one; the only other is too old and sick now. They can't go far, only far enough to see the edge of the light that fills the mine. They have to stop and find the name of one who can hear . . .

One?

One of the workers in Deep Salt. There are few who can. But when there is one, the guide can call him.

Could you speak with your father, the way we speak? Danatok said.

No, Hari said. Not like I can with horses and Tealeaf and Pearl. But sometimes Tarl seemed to hear and something came back, like a kind of whisper.

It might be enough.

Why can't we go now?

Because Danatok isn't well enough from last time, when he brought out one who died. He's still sick from the light and musn't go yet, Teelar said.

Mother, Danatok said, it is passing. I feel it leave. I'll be all right. And this man Tarl – he hasn't been there long, only a few days, and if I can bring him out he has a chance. He mightn't die.

Do they all die? The ones you save? Hari said.

Yes, sooner or later. The sickness from the light they work in wastes them away.

Why do you save them, then?

So they can die peacefully, not as slaves, Gantok said. It's all we can do. But we have few guides. Only Danatok now.

How many have you brought out? Pearl said.

Not many. Nine. Ten. Tarl will be eleven, if I can find him.

What about all the others sent to work there? No one ever comes back from Deep Salt, Hari said.

They wander away when the sickness becomes too great. They lie down in the caves and die.

And you get sick too?

My son recovers, Teelar said. But he mustn't go into the light. Or go too often. Or too soon.

When? Hari said.

Not tomorrow. The morning after, Tealeaf said.

How?

By boat. But now, we've promised Pearl an answer to her questions.

Can I go with Hari to save his father? Pearl said. She was filled with shame that her people, Company, sent slaves to work in Deep Salt, where they died. She must be no part of it, and helping Hari find his father seemed a way of showing where she stood.

All the same, she was relieved when Tealeaf said: No, Pearl. The more who go, the greater the danger. And there's only room in the boat for two and the one they save. Hari and Danatok will be gone for five days. You'll stay with me. There are things I want to teach you in that time.

Then start now. Tell me why you brought me here.

It's a simple story, Pearl, but not easy to understand. First you have to know who Dwellers are. Gantok tells it best. Listen . . .

The old Dweller composed his face, self-importantly Pearl thought, like her father whenever he had anything to say. Then his voice strode into the silence as though he were singing: The land is vast, the sea is vast, they breathe the air we breathe. There is no this thing and that thing, Pearl and Hari. All is one. Land, air, water, wind and sky, plants that spring from soil and rock, animals in the forest, fish in the sea, birds in the air, and humans in all their different colours and shapes. This is all we know, a simple thing and enough, which every child understands as soon as he is born. You, Hari, knew it, and you Pearl, but have forgotten. Unless the knowledge is taken with first breath and drunk thereafter with mother's milk . . .

'Where,' Hari said – said with a snarl – 'in Blood Burrow? Where would I see plants and fish and birds? And breathe air that didn't stink of piss and shit?'

'Hari, Hari,' Tealeaf said.

'He doesn't know what he's talking about. I never drank any mother's milk. She never had any, she was too starved. My father had to trap a bitch who'd lost her pups. I had dog's milk or I would have died.' He kicked the dog lying at his feet, making it yelp. 'But that doesn't make them my brothers. I kill them or they kill me.'

'There's no blame, Hari. Gantok isn't blaming you.'

'He'd better not.'

Gantok was smiling. No blame, he said. And no praise for Dwellers. We're the way we are by good fortune. The old story says we were mistaken many times, but heard the voice and learned to know through times that began when we lived in the trees, and we're learning still, and no doubt, Hari, remain mistaken about many things.

'Company came,' Hari said. 'That's all I know. That's what Lo taught me.'

'I don't want to hear about Company,' Pearl said. 'I want to know why you brought us here.'

'Gantok will tell you,' Tealeaf said.

But, said the old Dweller politely, let me finish what I was saying first, otherwise I'll lose my thread. His silent voice took on its singing notes, but in a less pronounced way, perhaps out of nervousness that Hari would burst into another snarl.

The land is vast . . .

'You told us,' Hari said.

When you stood on the mountains on your way here, Tealeaf – her name, you know, is Xantee, but let it pass – Tealeaf showed it to you, stretching away north and east. It goes on to the shores of the Inland Sea, then on again to another great sea, but if you tried to walk there, Pearl, through the jungles, over the plains and over the mountain ranges, it would take you as many years as you have been alive.

'If she didn't get eaten by fangcats on the way,' Hari said.

Beyond the sea, which no boat we know of has ever crossed, the voice tells us of another great land, and beyond that another and then another sea, with all creatures, human, animal, bird and fish, living there. Northwards there are ice lands, glaciers and rivers, islands of ice floating in the sea, and creatures again living there. Humans too. Not Dwellers. Not your races, Pearl and Hari. And south, far south, beyond many lands burnt by the sun and other lands of jungle and mountain and desert, there is ice again. That is the world.

'You've left out west,' Hari said. 'Where Company comes from.'

And everywhere, Gantok went on, sing-song still and unperturbed, everything is in harmony, and all races know the thing we know, that all is one – land, sea, air . . .

'Rats, dogs, Company clerks,' Hari said.

Gantok fell silent. After a moment he said: Yes, Hari,

you're right. Company clerks. And men with hands that burn other men. So, let us turn our eyes over the sea that lies beyond our beach to the land in the west where they come from. But remember your own race too, Hari, that built a city before Company came, and learned greed and how to take too much, and remember Cowl who would be king.

'Lo told me all that.'

Lo, yes, one who could speak?

He taught me.

You have told Xantee – Tealeaf – about him?

Yes, Tealeaf said. A speaker. And there must have been others.

He showed me how to talk with rats and horses. And dogs. I'm sorry I kicked you, dog.

The dog, off in a corner, thumped its tail on the wall.

And Lo knew the story of Company and Cowl, and the return of Company?

All that. But he didn't know about where they came from.

A great land, a vast land, Gantok said. (He seemed to like saying vast, Pearl thought.) And the people there, the humans, ambitious to be rich and to rule. All other races must bow down and serve. There were no Dwellers there, and no Dwellers, not even Sunderlok, ever travelled over that wide sea, but we have learned much of the place from Xantee, who lived in your city quietly, hidden away, for many years, Pearl, before she met you and became Tealeaf, your servant.

Tealeaf, were you a spy? Pearl said.

I was sent to learn and send word back. It was time we knew, Tealeaf said.

Company, Gantok said, she taught us Company. And now we have learned that its greed has destroyed it, over the sea. It has fallen apart; the laws and structures have crumbled and are gone, according to this boy, Kyle-Ott, who hunted you on your way. Too much oppression. Too much misery. The people rose up and destroyed it. Centuries must pass before some new order takes its place. A thousand petty rulers, a thousand creeds, so I would guess, all set on greater conquest and greater wealth, until some new Company rises again, and so it will go on in the way your races, Hari and Pearl, seem to desire.

'Are you blaming us?' Hari said.

Unless, Gantok said, ignoring him, someone there can learn and someone hear the voice.

'What, land and sea and winds and sky? That voice?' Hari said.

Some hear it whisper, Hari. One or two amongst us. And the people with no name, in the jungles, they hear. But although Company lies in ruins over the sea, the cycle will come round again and there will be huge armies, and conquest and massacre again and fleets on the seas with their cannons, and riches again, and starvation again, and factories pouring out smoke that kills the air, and poisoned rivers, poisoned seas and a dead land.

'We'll have that here,' Hari said. 'With Ottmar and his son. He's not going to close his factories just because he calls himself king instead of Company. He'll be worse.'

We know that, Hari, Tealeaf said. Already the forests outside the city are gone. Company has done that. And south, for hundreds of leagues, trees are felled. There will be a pause now while this Ottmar makes his rule secure, but then he'll start again. As you say, he is king and Company too.

But there's a greater danger, Gantok said.

I don't want to hear it, Pearl said. She felt forlorn. She felt lonely – all this talk of armies and destruction seemed like a storm raging around a house in which she sat huddled in a corner, feeling windows shake and walls heave. Yet she was expected to do something about it, when all she had asked for was an answer to her question . . .

She spoke aloud, and was comforted by the sound of her voice. 'Tealeaf, how did you find me? And what do you want me to do?'

Ah, Pearl, nothing yet. In a little while . . .

'Did you come to the city to see if there was someone like me?'

I came to read the danger more closely. But also, yes, to see if there might be someone of your race who had taken the step Dwellers have taken . . .

'How to speak?' She repeated it silently: How to speak?

Yes, that. And then perhaps taken the step beyond. It seemed to us that if the seed was there, even a tiny seed, even with just one of you, then there was hope. Your race might be ready for the next step, and might hear – well, Gantok has told you what you might hear. So I waited and I listened and heard nothing for many years.

She was chosen for this task, Gantok said, because among Dwellers Xantee is the one who hears best.

Tealeaf shook her head to silence him. I lived in the city, she said, among the workers, with people like Tilly, and then in the mansions as a kitchen maid.

I'll bet you didn't come to Blood Burrow, Hari said.

No, Hari, not there.

Or the port. You might have heard Lo. He could speak.

I wish I'd met Lo. But instead I worked as a street sweeper in the fashionable part of the town. I was sweeping the gutter one day outside a milliner's shop when a carriage drew up. The coachman struck me with his whip to move me out of the way. Then a footman lowered the steps and helped a lady and a child down. They went into the shop. Something

121

about the child attracted me – the way she moved, the way she would not let her mother hurry her. I waited, nursing the welt on my cheek the coachman's whip had made. When the woman and the girl came out, a beggar girl was passing. Beggars, as you know, Pearl, are forbidden in that part of City. She was slinking along by the wall, but the child saw her. You saw her, Pearl, and you told your mother to wait, and you felt in your purse for a coin. Your mother scolded you and told you to come, and you said: Wait, mother, and she stood still. I heard you speak, and you did not know it. You did not know you hadn't spoken aloud. You gave the beggar a coin and followed your mother into the coach, where she scolded you properly as you drove away. And a Whip came by and burned the beggar girl with his gloves and moved me on too. But I had read the emblem on the door of the coach – House Bowles. So, Pearl . . .

You came to our house and told me to choose you as my maid.

Yes.

You taught me. You saved me from marrying Ottmar.

'If you'd married him you'd be a queen by now,' Hari said. He grinned at her. 'You'd be boss.'

Be quiet, Pearl ordered, making him wince, then finger his knife. She turned to Tealeaf: Now I'm here, what do you want me to do?

I don't know. The council doesn't know. You're safe. And I found Hari on the way . . .

'I found you,' Hari muttered.

So, there are two, one from each race in the city. And there was Lo, Hari tells us. So it seems – it seems as if something is beginning. There's hope. But what we do, I don't know.

'I know,' Hari said. 'I get my father out of Deep Salt. Danatok, can you show me this boat we'll sail in?'

Yes, Danatok said. My father's boat. I've sailed with him since I was able to stand. Come with me. I'll teach you.

They left the house and went down to the creek mouth and along the beach to where the boats were drawn up.

Can you swim? Danatok said.

Better than you, Hari said.

He helped Danatok pull the little boat down to the sea, and watched and listened as the boy, moving with agility and sureness, hauled up a small square sail and guided the boat out through the waves. They sailed back and forth between the headlands, then out to sea until the village shrank to a cluster of grey huts. Danatok taught Hari to set the sail and steer with the tiller.

You learn quickly, he said.

In the burrows you learn or die, Hari said. Does Company come here?

No. There's no profit for them. They sail past. Once a war boat stopped and fired guns and knocked down houses. They planted a flag on the beach to show we belonged to them. Ottmar's flag. The same that flies over the salt mines. The salt mines are south. But one day, when everything is poisoned, in Ottmar's time or someone else's, they'll turn their eyes this way.

Danatok shivered. Hari shivered too, but told himself it was because the wind was springing up. They guided the boat back to the beach, where the dog was waiting.

Can he come with us when we go? Hari said.

Why not? There's room.

They pulled the boat up on the sand.

We'll sail again tomorrow and leave at dawn the next day, Danatok said. Now I'm tired. I've got to rest.

He walked away, small and frail, like the burrows-children who never grew. Hari wondered what the sickness was and if it had struck Tarl yet, and why Danatok risked so much to save a man he had never met. He wondered if he risked getting the sickness himself.

EIGHT

They sailed at dawn on Hari's third day in Stone Creek, with Pearl and Tealeaf watching from the beach and the dog shivering in the bow. A waterproof sack held food for five days. A small skin of water was tied to the mast. They would go ashore and take more from streams when they needed it, Danatok said. His mother did not come to see them off, but Hari heard the silent murmur of their goodbyes.

On the first night they slept under trees at a river mouth, wrapped in thin blankets Danatok pulled from a locker in the bow. They had sailed past headlands and cliffs and the lumpy end of a mountain range but seen no villages or people. The second day took them by taller cliffs and black reefs. Danatok kept them closer to shore, saying that Company scows were sometimes driven this way by unfavourable tides as they tried to make the harbour at Saltport.

'Where's the mine?' Hari said.

'See the big mountain that looks like a shaved head? It's high up there, half a day's journey inland. There's a railway running down to the port. The miners bring the salt out, trucks carry it down, the full ones pull the empty ones up. The miners live in huts at the mouth of the mine. Other workers load the ships in the port. They stay until they're too old to work. I don't know what Company does with them after that.'

'They die,' Hari said. 'No one ever comes back. Where's Deep Salt?'

'Deep Salt.' Danatok shivered. 'It's not part of the salt mine. It's something different.'

'Further away?'

'No, closer. See where the mountains touch the sea? There are three hills, two of them with trees and one in the middle, bare.'

'A grey one,' Hari said. It was scaly and crusted, and hurt his eyes where sunlight reflected off sheets of rock.

'That's Deep Salt. House Ottmar has worked the salt mines since Company first came, but no one went near the bare hill. All they knew about it was it made men sick. No animals went near. No plants grew there. But Ottmar, this Ottmar who calls himself king, grew curious, so he sent slaves to mine it. It didn't matter how many died. They tunnelled in and found what they found.'

'Salt tigers,' Hari said.

Danatok smiled. 'Not salt tigers. They don't exist. And no deep pit to the centre of the world, sucking down the souls of men. They found what poisoned the hill. That's what they dig for now.'

'What is it?'

'I don't know. None of the slaves we've brought out have a name for it.'

'What does it do to them?'

'It turns their skin white. Their skin will tear like paper. It makes them bleed, with blood like water – so thin, once it starts it never stops. Their bones burst through their skin and break like rotten branches on a tree.'

'But Tarl has only been there a day or two. How long does it take?' Hari cried.

'I brought out a man who had been there half a year. He died before we got home to the village. Another – half that time. He lived, then died.'

'So Tarl should be all right?'

'I hope so, Hari. We'll see. Now, pull that rope and trim the sail. It's three hours till dark and I want to be tied up by then.'

'By Deep Salt?'

'Close by. Pull harder. The wind's getting up.'

They sailed on, as close to the reefs as Danatok dared, then turned into a bite in the land, sailing in shadow as the sun sank low. The mountains angled east and south, with wind-flattened trees clinging to rocky faces, then stepped back, exposing the inland one of the trio of hills. It was round and green, an ordinary hill rimmed with pebble beaches and white breaking waves. They went past on a softer breeze. The middle hill butted into the sea. It looked, Hari thought, like a head covered with warts and scabs, and sunken scars that shone silvery although no light reached them, and sockets where eyes had been gouged out. Danatok sailed hard, urging the boat past. They came to the seaward hill, which seemed to waft clean air from its trees, and Hari breathed a sigh of relief as the boat glided into a little bay with a stony beach. The dog jumped out. Hari followed and held the bow steady as Danatok lowered the sail. He tied a loop of rope round a tree branch. They ate a quick meal, then Danatok said, 'I want to go over the hill and see what's happening on the other side.'

He took a torch of bound twigs from the locker, struck sparks on it from a tinder, and soon it burned softly, a small fist of light. They set off through the trees at the back of the beach, leaving the dog guarding the boat. Hari, who liked to lead or else be alone, followed the Dweller boy, who knew so much more than him and had abilities he would never equal. But, he thought, wait till we have to fight someone. He smiled to himself. They climbed through tangled ferns and tree trunks for an hour, and slowly a rumbling sound grew and the sky lightened beyond the hill. Without noticing it, they began to speak silently.

The port's working. They're loading salt, Danatok said. But usually it's noisier than this. He pushed the torch handle into soft ground. We'll leave it here. They might see.

They crept on, and soon the hill flattened, then sloped down. They crouched in the ferns and looked at Saltport. A long wharf jutted into the sea, with sheds at its base and a cluster of buildings – houses, a few shops and offices – further inland. A double railway line ran over a plain, then up a low hill rising at the base of the mountains. It climbed almost sheer to a plateau where huts for miners stood in rows. The mouth of the mine opened beyond, glowing with light.

There were no trains on the railway, but at the port men pushed carts along the wharf to a ship flying the Ottmar flag. The wheels made the rumbling they had heard. A steam crane lifted the carts and poured white salt into the ship's hold.

Danatok frowned. There's usually two or three ships, he said. And the mine isn't working. There are no trains coming down.

Because, Hari said, guessing, there's fighting back in the city. Ottmar probably hasn't made himself king properly yet. And there's nowhere to send his salt, not with Company over the sea broken up. I've seen his salt ships leaving Port three at a time.

Then I wonder if Deep Salt's working, Danatok said.

Where is it?

In answer, as though he was afraid of speaking, Danatok pointed into the night, round to their left, where the light from the lamps alongside the railroad failed to reach, and Hari saw a white fuzz, like a puff of smoke held still and lit from behind. It came from a single light on a post beside the stumpy end of the grey hill he had seen from the sea. A small hut stood below the light, with a watchman sitting in front of it, seeming to sleep.

That? Hari said. Just that hut?

Look at the hill.

Hari strained his eyes at the stumpy shape and in a moment saw a deeper greyness, not large at this distance, no larger than the watchman's hut.

A door? he said.

An iron door. That's the way into Deep Salt. It's wide enough for one man, and they never open it except to let new workers in. Nothing comes out. No workers, ever again. And nothing they mine in there comes out. There must be a rail inside, going into the hill. They open an iron shutter and put food and water on a trolley and push it in. Then they close the shutter. And that's all.

How do I know if Tarl's inside?

Twenty days since he was taken. He'll be there. But if we're lucky, he hasn't been long.

Long enough for the sickness? Hari whispered.

I don't know.

Let's go then. I'll fix the guard. Hari loosened his knife in its sheath.

No. That entrance can't be opened except by a clerk from Saltport with two keys. We go back over the hill.

Then what?

You'll see.

They went back to the torch, which still burned softly in its knotted twigs, and made their way down to the beach, where the dog, whining and writhing, welcomed them.

Stay here, dog. Look after the boat, Danatok said. Follow me, Hari.

They clambered over rocks at the end of the beach, wading here and there, then climbed partway up the cliff and down again.

Now we swim, Danatok said. I hope your father can swim.

He sank into the water and swam on his side, with one arm holding the torch out of the sea. Hari followed. They came to a hollow in the cliff, with water booming faintly inside.

The back way into Deep Salt, Danatok said. There are caves and pits all over the place. It took us a long time to find it. Only one passage leads to the mine, where they dig for whatever it is.

How long to get there?

Half the night. The other half to bring him out. Hari, wait here. There's no need for you to get close to the light.

No, I'm coming. I told Tarl I would. He's my father.

You might get the sickness too.

Then I'll get it. Come on, let's go.

He was more afraid than he showed, but he would not let this boy take all the risk – and if Tarl died, then Hari wanted to die. No I don't, he thought, I want to kill someone, I want to kill Ottmar.

The wish was so strong that Danatok recoiled from him.

I thought Xantee said you had a dream about not killing, he said. Anyway, there's no one here to kill. You might find rats, though. Save your knife for them.

He held the torch high and led Hari into the cave. They climbed on ledges, swam across the mouths of narrow caves

130

leading into darkness. Danatok was quick and sure. The way became easier but did not always follow the widest path. When Hari asked where the side-caves went, Danatok did not know, but said there were pools in some that went down forever. He watched the torch anxiously and blew on it several times to ignite another in the tangle of iron-hard twigs in its core.

What happens if it goes out? Hari said.

We die.

I can find my way back. I've memorised it.

The rats won't let you.

Yes, I can feel them. Hear them too – a rustle of claws on stone, a sliding of greasy fur along stone walls. He saw too, in a moment, a flashing of red eyes, half a dozen pairs, beyond the torchlight.

The light keeps them off. They hate the torch because of the other light, in the mine, Danatok said.

Why don't they die like the miners?

It works on them another way. It makes them grow in strange shapes. I've seen a rat here with two heads. And one with ears all along its back. Ah, a new skeleton, he got a long way.

Danatok held the torch over the white bones of a man.

When they die of the sickness, he said, the other miners carry out their bodies for the rats to pick clean. Others wander away and lie down and die, like this one here, and the rats eat their flesh. You'll see more skeletons soon. Come on, Hari. We're nearly at the centre of the hill. My torch is half burned. We'll have to hurry.

They passed more skeletons, some yellowed with age. Skulls, hair, rags of clothing lay scattered on the stone. Some of these men, Hari thought, had come from Blood Burrow. He might have known them. Then the darkness grew less intense. Light, faintly green, made a thin dilution of the black.

Far enough, Danatok said. This is where I call those who can hear.

I want to see, Hari said.

You can't. I've never seen. Even this much light makes my skin feel as if ants are crawling on it. Do you feel it?

Hari did – a prickling and itching as though a wind was blowing chips of glass against his skin.

The place where they dig is another ten minutes' walk. I have to stand and listen for a while before I can hear someone's name inside his head. Then I call him. Sometimes there aren't any. But we know Tarl, if he can hear.

Say his name, Hari said.

Hold the torch.

He gave it to Hari, closed his eyes, turned up his face, concentrated. Hari heard the name chime out, making no sound, and move like a wind blowing into the dark: Tarl! Tarl!

They waited.

He doesn't answer, Danatok said.

Keep trying.

Danatok held himself still, and spoke again. Hari saw how all his strength was concentrated into the cry: Tarl! Say your name, Tarl.

No, I feel nothing. Unless he hears, he can't follow. Hari, the torch will die if we don't start back soon.

Let me try. I can make him hear, Hari said.

Yes, try. Be quick.

Hari gave Danatok the torch. He stepped a little forward, away from the boy, and thought for a moment: his father in Blood Burrow, hunting king rats in the ruins, with Hari, two years old, clinging to his back, and the pair of them sitting in a shattered room, under broken beams, roasting rat legs on the embers of a fire, and Tarl tearing tender meat from the bones and feeding it into his son's mouth – my mouth, Hari thought, my father; and he drew the memory into the shape of Tarl's black-bladed knife and hurled it towards the green light; and followed it with a shriller, purer cry: Tarl, my father, I am here. Follow my voice.

Nothing for moment. Then a whisper, far off, in the dark: Hari? My son?

Tarl, I told you I'd come. Follow my voice. Come quickly. We don't have much time.

Keep calling, Hari, Danatok said.

Quiet, Hari said, concentrating.

Tarl, he repeated, I'm here. This is your name. Follow it. Close your eyes. Walk along your name like a path. Tarl. Tarl.

He kept up the call, making it ring like a bell from him to his father. It began to exhaust him, but Danatok put his hand on his shoulder, feeding his own strength into him, and soon they heard a shuffling of steps and saw a faint movement, like a shadow, in the light.

Hari raised his voice in a shout: 'Tarl!'

'Hari, Hari,' came the whispered reply. Tarl came limping, shuffling, into the torchlight: Tarl barefooted, with outstretched arms and wild eyes, wearing only a scrap of cloth round his loins.

Hari ran forward and caught him in his arms, and thought for a moment that sickness had shrunk him, but it was Tarl sinking to his knees. His tears soaked Hari's doublet. Soft choking cries came from his mouth.

'Hari, you can't be here. There's no way. I had – no hope. When I saw the place – and felt the filthy light inside me – crawling like worms . . .'

'Tarl, there's a back way out. Danatok showed me. Stand

up. We've got to go. There are rats all around us. If the torch goes out . . .' He raised his father: 'Come on. Walk.'

'I can't . . .'

'You can. Tarl the Hunter. Gather your strength. We've got a boat.'

'And the sea is waiting,' Danatok said. 'We'll wash you clean.'

He led the way, holding the torch high. Hari brought Tarl, making him walk, hauling him up when he stumbled, making him half run when the way was smooth. The torch grew dim. There were hundreds of red eyes in the dark, and a chittering of hundreds of rat voices. They'll have the flesh off us before we can scream, Hari thought, and he cried at Danatok and Tarl to go faster. But the sound of rats, a sound he knew, seemed to revive Tarl, and he moved more surely, with greater strength.

'I need my knife,' he said.

'Here, Tarl.' Hari drew it from its sheath and forced it into his father's hand. Tarl's fingers closed on the hilt, and he stood straighter, and Hari felt him turn into Tarl the hunter again.

'How big are these rats?'

'As big as Hari's dog, some of them,' Danatok said.

'King rats,' said Tarl. 'Stop when you get to a narrow place.'

'They'll kill us.'

'Do what he says,' Hari said.

They reached an opening where only one could pass at a time. Danatok stopped and let the others through, then ran after them in the dying light.

'Now let my father stand in the opening,' Hari said.

'And take the light away, but not too far,' Tarl said. 'Just enough for me to see their eyes.'

Danatok and Hari went another half dozen steps, and the
rats beyond the gap slid at Tarl in a shallow wave of black and
brown fur and purple eyes and yellow teeth. His knife moved
too fast for Hari to see, and a spray of blood shot up his arm.
Rats screamed, but one, a giant, hairless and pink, slid past
Tarl's legs and sank its teeth into his calf muscle. Hari jumped
forward and broke its back with a heel kick.

'Tarl, enough. Come on.'

Danatok thrust the torch into the gap, making enough
light to push the rats back.

'Seven,' Tarl said, 'and one to you, Hari. They'll feed on
the bodies and not follow for a while. How far?'

'Close enough. Smell the sea,' Danatok said.

'I smell only blood and that filthy stuff in the mine. Hurry,
boy. I've got no more strength.'

Hari supported him again and found that Tarl had spoken
the truth, his strength was gone, and it was only the knife,
clasped in his hand, that told him who he was – the knife
and me, Hari thought, Hari, his son. The knowledge that they
would come out of Deep Salt elated him. Then he thought:
Safe except for the sickness, and he supported his father
anxiously, feeling Tarl weaken with every step.

The torch died with a sputter, and the scraping of rat
claws, the rushing of rat bodies, grew again. Hari tried to
force them back with his mind, but they were too many.
Danatok plunged on, running, swimming cave mouths,
finding his way from memory, and at last Hari saw a point of
light in the blackness – a star shining in the sky, a star in the
world outside Deep Salt.

'Tarl, we're nearly there. The rats won't follow. We're out
of Deep Salt.'

Hari half threw, half lifted Tarl into the sea, dragged him
out from the rocks, with Danatok swimming at his side. The

rat squeals faded. The gentle slap of water and the whisper of a breeze took their place. Hari and Danatok swam, floating Tarl between them on his back. They rounded the bulge in the cliff and came to the beach, where they washed Tarl in the shallows, scrubbing him with pebbles and sand. They scrubbed themselves, trying to get rid of the itching that had crept on their skin since they had stood at the edge of the green light. The dog ran back and forth on the beach, whimpering.

'Tarl, let me take the knife.'

'No. It remembers me. I'll hold it.'

They sat him in water up to his waist, pulled the boat beside him, heaved him in, threw in the dog. Dawn was in the sky, making the clouds bleed. Everything is blood, Hari thought. He felt sick.

'Let's get out of this place.'

They sailed straight out to sea, then tacked north. Tarl lay shivering in the bow. He could scarcely speak. 'Cold. Cold,' he mumbled.

'He has the sickness,' Danatok said.

'How long were you in Deep Salt, Tarl?' Hari said.

'There's no time there.' He leaned over the side, retching, but nothing came from his mouth.

Hari pulled blankets from the locker. He wrapped them round Tarl, then tried to make him drink and eat, but Tarl could not.

'Cold,' he whispered.

'Come here, dog,' Hari said. He lifted the animal on top of Tarl. 'Lie there. Keep him warm.'

'The dog will get sick too,' Danatok said.

Hari took no notice, and the dog appeared happy enough, seeming to find comfort in Tarl.

They sailed all that day, turned into a creek mouth at

nightfall, made a fire, and all that time Tarl slept, and dreamed, and woke and cried out hoarsely, hugging the dog to his chest. Hari and Danatok spent the night by the fire, sleeping as well as they could without blankets. In the morning they went on. Tarl stayed the same, and the dog did not need to be told to curl against him. He lay with his head on Tarl's chest, and Hari thought: Tarl has him now. He's Tarl's dog. The knife was Tarl's too, held in his fist.

With the wind behind them they reached the village at nightfall; and Hari saw, as Danatok steered the boat to the beach, that the boy had hardly any strength left. He too was sick, though not as badly as Tarl. For himself, Hari was tired from lack of sleep and hard sailing. The itch was gone from his body. It was as if the wind and sea had washed him clean.

Pearl and Tealeaf and half a dozen Dwellers waited on the beach. Men lifted Tarl onto a stretcher. The dog snapped at their hands when they tried to lift him clear, so they let him stay. They carried the stretcher up the beach.

'Where are they taking him?' Hari said.

'To the sickhouse. They'll nurse him,' Tealeaf said. 'No, Hari, don't go. You can see him in a few days. We've seen men from Deep Salt worse than your father.'

'Danatok?' He looked for the boy, and saw his mother helping him towards the village.

'He's all right. We've seen him worse too.'

'I wouldn't have found Tarl without him.'

Danatok, he called.

The boy turned.

Thank you.

Danatok smiled, raised his hand, and his mother led him away.

Hari, Pearl said, what's Deep Salt?

137

'I don't want to talk about it. It's sick. A sick place. I'll –'
He looked in her face, saw her concern and, with wonder,
realised it was for him. He felt as if he had stepped off a
ledge and was falling. Tarl had been concerned for him. And
Lo. But no one else, ever.

I'll tell you, he said. But now I need to sleep. I'll tell you
tomorrow.

Yes. Tomorrow, Pearl said.

NINE

Dweller children were teaching her to swim. There had been perfumed baths at home, with maids soaping her. That had been the only touch of water she had known. It was not thought proper for Company women to swim. But with naked children frolicking around her in the creek, Pearl learned quickly and soon was jumping from the bank and turning and twisting in the depths, picking coloured stones from the bottom. She made little mounds of them on the grass and thought they were prettier than the necklaces and rings in the jewel box she had left behind in her dressing room. And all the time she swam, or walked by herself on the beach, or lay in bed waiting for sleep, there seemed to be a soft voice at her ear whispering: Pearl.

Who are you? she wondered. What do you want me to do?

She asked Tealeaf, who smiled and touched her on the forehead: There's nothing to do, Pearl, except wait.

I heard it say my name when we were in the jungle.

Yes, I know.

Do you hear it?

It speaks to me, but not as clearly as to you. And saying your name might be all it will ever do.

Pearl seemed to understand that in a way it was enough, this breathing of her name. It soon became as natural as the beating of her heart, and although it was always there she was rarely conscious of it. She wondered if Hari heard it too – his name – and thought, a little smugly, that he did not, that he would always be too busy to listen.

She had missed him while he was away. She had worried about him. It was not that she liked him; she did not, because he was too rough and too ugly, with his scars and red-black skin and hair hanging matted down his back, but they spoke to each other, in their minds, and seemed to touch as naturally as breathing, even when he was angry and hating her – as naturally as this new voice whispering in her ear. So when he was gone it was like feeling a cold patch on her skin.

Hari, she said, sitting by the creek alone, come and tell me about Deep Salt.

There was no answer, and she supposed that although it was late in the morning he was still sleeping off his tiredness.

She had not liked the look of Tarl as he had been lifted onto the stretcher: his face was even more scarred than Hari's, from rat bites, she supposed, and disfigured by the number burned on his forehead. He held Hari's knife as though he meant never to let it go. She had a sick realisation of the life they must have led, Tarl and Hari, in the ruined city, in Blood Burrow, fighting, killing, living on what they could scavenge, while she . . . Pearl did not want to think about it. She stood up and stripped off her clothes and dived into the creek. Deep down, she hunted for coloured stones. If her mother could see her now, and her sister . . . She almost laughed, and lost half her air and scrambled for the surface, where she thought: My mother and sister are murdered by Ottmar. All my family are dead.

She sat on the bank, thinking about them. There had been no love – no one had ever said 'love' – so she did not cry, but she felt a deep sorrow for them. It was as though only part of them had been alive – her father's eyes, judging and cold; her mother's tongue, scolding; her sister's laugh, always scornful or dissatisfied; her brothers' . . . She thought of Hubert, killed by Hari. The knife that Tarl held so tightly now had gone into his throat. She was glad that Hari no longer had it.

Heard you calling, Hari's voice said in her head.

He was standing behind her.

She grabbed her clothes and pulled them on, while he watched, grinning.

You're white like those muggy grubs, he said.

She did not think he meant it as an insult. He was simply stating a fact.

And you're brown, she said. The first time I saw you I thought it was dirt. And she thought: Some of it was. But he had never had servants washing him. Or dressing him and serving him with food. Had he even known each morning when he woke if he would eat anything that day?

Tell me about Deep Salt, she said.

Surprisingly, he shivered, and a look of fear crossed his face.

I'm trying to forget that place.

I heard my brothers talking about it once. They said Ottmar mines it for jewels that explode in the sun, so he can never bring them out, it's too dangerous. But one day he'll find a way. Did you see the jewels?

I didn't see anything. It was dark. Then we came to the light and we stopped . . .

Tell me.

She sat down, inviting him to sit beside her. He squatted instead and took stones from one of her mounds and lobbed them one by one into the creek. She saw how accurately he threw, with each stone following the curve of the one before and hitting the water in the same place. She would not have been surprised if they made another neat pile on the bottom.

Tell me about how you sailed there, for a start.

With Danatok. I wouldn't have found my father without him.

He began to describe it, haltingly at first, then in a voice that sounded hushed and horrified: sailing down the coast, the three hills with a dead one in the middle, the port and the salt mine, the iron door. And the caverns after that, endless and black, with Danatok's torch making a pool of light that shrank and shrank. He told her about the skeletons and the rats.

Then my skin started to itch. And we saw the green light, and Danatok said we couldn't go any further.

He told her how he had called his father and how Tarl had come, and they had run, while the rats that had followed them parted and let them through, held off by the torchlight, and then began to follow again, coming closer as the light began to fade, until they were nipping at their heels.

Giant rats, he said. One with two heads and one with tails growing out of its back, and some with long white hair and some with no hair at all.

Pearl saw tears running down his face.

Rats shouldn't be like that, he said.

Why are they? What does it?

It must be what they mine in Deep Salt. The thing that makes you sick and makes you die. The rats can live with it if they don't go too close, but it changes them . . .

And kills the men? But Hari, you could have stopped the rats. You can do it with horses and the dog. With people too. You could have told them to stay back.

'Do you think I didn't try?' he cried, hurting her ears. Then more softly, and silently: I tried. But I was helping Tarl and I couldn't concentrate; I couldn't speak to more than one at a time and they kept on coming. So I tried to make a wall they couldn't get through; I thought that would stop them, but it was full of holes and they came wriggling . . . So we ran. They would have got us if Tarl hadn't killed some with my knife. His knife. They stopped to feed on the dead ones, and then they came again, and the torch went out. But we got to the entrance and saw the stars, and it was the starlight that stopped them. I've never seen anything so . . . Does Tealeaf know about stars? I want to know. What are they? What are their names?

Tealeaf knows everything. But I can tell you, Hari. She taught me.

Danatok uses the stars when he's sailing the boat.

Hari wiped the tears from his face.

We washed my father. We tried to wash the sickness off. We used the dog to keep him warm. The dog is his now. He's called Dog. We brought him home. You know the rest. He's in the sickhouse. They won't let me in but they say he'll be all right. Two days. Three. Then he can come out.

And he'll tell us what they do in Deep Salt, Pearl said. Tealeaf says none of the men they've brought out before have been able to talk about it. They just kept quiet and then they died. But Tarl was only there for a day or two, Tealeaf thinks.

It made him sick, like a starving dog. I thought he was dying. First he was cold, then he was hot, he shivered all over and said his skin was coming off . . .

But he's all right, Pearl said. Hari, he'll live.

Yes, he'll live. I did what I promised. I saved Tarl.

He sat brooding on the bank, then suddenly jumped up, stripped off his clothes and dived into the creek. She saw him swimming deep down, undulating like the animal that had swum off the beach yesterday – a seal. She wondered if her voice would reach him underwater.

Hari, she said.

He surfaced: What?

Just trying it out.

He sank to the bottom: Pearl.

Yes, it works. Hari, will you teach me to sail the boat?

When?

Now.

He came to the surface and dressed on the bank, turning his back when he saw her watching. She had never seen a naked man before, or a naked person of any sort, except for herself in mirrors, until those Dweller children yesterday. She thought Hari was not so ugly without his clothes, and those parts she had never seen before, but sometimes imagined, were curious and interesting.

They went down to the beach and launched the boat Danatok and he had used, and for two days he taught her to sail, and learned to sail better himself. On the second afternoon the breeze died. They drifted off the beach, watching people walking in the village and working in the gardens further back, on the gentle slopes. The blue hills rose beyond, range on range, and far-away mountains with snowy peaks shone in the sun.

Trees, Hari said. I never saw trees in Blood Burrow. When I saw one for the first time, in your garden . . .

Spying on me.

. . . I was afraid. I didn't know what it was or what it might

144

do. It might walk. It might pick me up in its branches and tear me open.

Was everything killing and blood?

Yes, everything. But when I was sure, I climbed into it and felt it growing inside itself. It was just being quiet and being itself. So I sat there with my arms around it, feeling it grow.

Hari, be quiet.

Why?

Be quiet a moment.

The boat rocked gently as the breeze came back and puffed the sail.

Do you hear anything? she said.

The mast creaking.

No. Something else.

What?

I hear something saying my name.

They waited, and she heard it – what was it? Did it matter? – say Pearl silently inside her, deep inside, in the folding places of her mind, and it was more than a name, and less than a welcome; it was a shifting over to make room for her, in the hills, in the trees, in the sea, and a shifting inside her, an exchange, to give room – and all as natural as breathing.

Hari?

Yes.

He felt it too. His name. His eyes went far away, into the hills, and darkened and grew deep as he made room.

They said nothing more. There was nothing to say. They sailed for the beach and hauled the boat onto the sand and walked to Sartok's house, where Tealeaf was waiting. She did not need to be told what had happened to them. But a look of deep contentment showed on her face, making her younger. She led them inside to the evening meal.

You can sail now, Pearl?

Yes. Hari showed me.

Why are you learning?

So that if we go back to City we can go that way and be quicker than going over the mountains.

Are you going back to City?

I don't know.

I'm going if Tarl wants to, Hari said.

Tarl will be out of the sickhouse tomorrow, Tealeaf said. He'll tell us what he wants to do.

And what he saw in Deep Salt, Pearl said.

Yes, what he saw there.

They ate their meal. Pearl and Hari were quiet. Deep Salt still made them afraid, but they were less afraid than before.

TEN

Tarl walked down from the sickhouse by himself. He wore new trousers and a shirt and doublet, and carried the black-bladed knife in a thong at his waist. Dog came at his side, staying so close his shoulder brushed Tarl's knee at every step.

Hari met his father at the door of the house by the creek. They clasped hands formally, then embraced.

'Tarl.'

'Hari, you came for me. I had no hope . . .'

'My friends helped me.'

Dog growled jealously at the closeness of the pair.

'These people, Hari? These Dwellers, what do they want?'

'Nothing, Tarl. They saved you because you could be saved. They saved me.'

'And now they want to know about Deep Salt.' A look of fear, a shudder, moved across his face as he spoke the name.

'You're well now,' Hari said, but he wasn't sure. Tarl's skin seemed looser, his hair was streaked with yellow and grey, and the black depths of his eyes had haunted movements, like creatures hiding deep in jungle trees.

'The council's waiting, Tarl. Come inside.'

Tealeaf and the old man, Gantok, sat at the table, with Pearl on a low stool by the window.

'Welcome, Tarl,' Gantok said. 'We're pleased to see you well.'

'Is this your council? Only two?'

'Our voices go out to everyone who wants to hear.'

'So it's true. Dwellers can speak without speech. I've heard of it but didn't believe it.'

'It's an ability we have,' Gantok said, in a satisfied way. 'Xantee is with me. It was she who brought your son from the city.'

Tarl's eyes fixed sharply on Tealeaf. Women took a lowly place in the burrows. 'Who's this?' he said then, looking at Pearl.

'She is Pearl. She came from the city too.'

Tarl's hand moved to his knife. 'She's Company.'

The dog growled.

Quiet, Dog, Pearl said, and it sank at Tarl's feet with a puzzled look.

'Hari,' Tarl said, 'she's Company. Company dies.' He drew his knife.

Hari stepped in front of him. 'No, Tarl. She's my friend.'

'Look at her white skin. Look at her eyes. Company has blue eyes. She dies.' He raised the knife.

Tarl, Tealeaf said softly.

He did not know where his name had come from. It held him motionless.

The knife is Dweller. It trembles in your hand. Put it away.

'You, woman? Is it you who tells me what to do?'

'Pearl has turned a corner from Company. Put your knife away. Tell your dog not to bare his teeth. We've nursed you.

148

Danatok, who carried the torch, lies sick still. Put off your own sickness. Put off your lust for blood.'

Pearl saw Tarl struggle for words and saw that his anger would break out again. She wasn't afraid. She would stop him easily. But she did not want to bully or command. Her mind today was like a cloth shaken out in the wind. Hari's was the same, she could tell, although he still had creases from his father.

She said, 'Tarl.'

'The girl speaks. No girl speaks until she's told.'

'Tarl,' she said, 'it's true, I was Company. But not any longer. I was House Bowles. Not any longer. I turned away from them and came here with Hari, and now I'm Pearl, nothing more.'

'I heard on the ship a girl from House Bowles was chosen for Ottmar's wife.'

'I ran away.'

'Ottmar of Deep Salt.' His hand tightened on his knife.

'And Ottmar is king now. The families are dead. My family too. Ottmar hunted me to be his slave. So don't hate me. The old ways are gone. There are new things to fight.'

'Pearl speaks the truth,' Gantok said. 'Put away your knife.'

Slowly, after a struggle, Tarl obeyed. The number burned on his forehead faded from red to white.

'Sit with us at the table. Tell us what you learned in Deep Salt.'

Tarl sat down. 'I am not,' he said haltingly. 'I do not want . . .'

'The place is terrible, we know.'

'First – you must tell me what's happening in the city. There's fighting there and Ottmar calls himself king. But what is happening in the burrows?'

149

'Dwellers are watching. They move in the shadows and no one sees. Xantee hears all they say to her.'

'What do they say?'

'It's true, Ottmar calls himself king, even though he's only Company with a new name. He's ruthless, he likes to kill, and he kills everyone who stands in his way. The families are dead. House Bowles is dead. But it's harder than he thinks. The cities in the south and east are in rebellion, and there are men there who also call themselves king. And in the city itself the clerks rose up and made an army, and then the workers rebelled and everyone fights everyone else and Ottmar's army can't crush them all. Some of the Whips too have rebelled. So Ottmar has long battles ahead.'

'But the burrows?' Tarl said.

'Yes, the burrows. They fight. There's a man called Keech . . .'

'From Keech Burrow. He's their best hunter.'

'And another called Keg . . .'

'From Keg Burrow.'

'Each leads his own band of hunters and they make raids in the city. The Whips don't dare go in the burrows any more. There are bands of women too, killing with knives.'

'From the Bawdhouse,' Tarl said. 'Who leads Blood Burrow?'

'We haven't heard. It will be many years before Ottmar can be the king he likes to call himself. But he is the strongest and will win. And they say he has a son, Kyle-Ott, a burned boy, who's even crueller than him. The city has bad days ahead.'

'No one leads Blood Burrow. There are none who could,' Tarl said. 'So Keech will try. He's tried before. I've got to go back.'

'No, Tarl,' Hari said.

'Hari, I've got to. There's something . . .' he turned to Gantok . . . 'something you must know. Keech isn't the only danger. I have to take the people of Blood Burrow away from there.'

'The danger comes from Deep Salt,' Tealeaf said.

'Yes. Deep Salt.'

'Then tell us, Tarl.'

His face seemed to collapse. It was as if his skin was not fixed to his flesh or his flesh properly to his bones. Dog crept under the table and lay across his feet.

'I can't find the words for it,' Tarl said.

'Then say no words. Remember, if you can, and let me take it from your mind.'

Shivering a little, he obeyed. He laid his trembling hands on the table and fixed his eyes on them as though seeing his own flesh might hold him together, and painfully, slowly, he brought out his memories for Tealeaf to see.

She spoke silently to the others, in Tarl's voice, with his burrows sound:

They took me, Tarl the Hunter, from People's Square, tied to a cart. They dragged me through back streets of the city to a barracks at the city wall. They gave the others clothes, but none for me. They gave them food, plain food, and a crust for me, because a Whip was dead and a clerk wounded. They said I was a savage and must be chained, and they chained me to another like me, a scrawny twisted fellow who spat and howled. He too was chosen for Deep Salt. They held us in a cell for four days, then marched us to Port and put us on a ship – one of Ottmar's ships. Others were there, going to the salt mines, but only I and Krog – that was his name, not a burrows man but a city man, taken for murder – were for Deep Salt. Krog spat and howled, but he howled from fear, for on the first night, in the cell where they kept us

151

apart from the rest, he made a loop in the chain and hanged himself on a spike fixed in the wall. He would rather have death than Deep Salt. I could have stopped him but I did not. If a man chooses to die, it's his own choice.

Hari made shallow breaths, with his eyes fixed on his father. Pearl sat bowed, with her hands hiding her eyes.

In the morning, when they found him, Tarl's voice, unsoftened by Tealeaf, went on, they carried him out and threw him over the side. I thought they meant to throw me as well, but they struck off my chains and tied me to the rail and flogged me and left me bleeding there. All day I stayed, with no water, and the sun beating down. But I am Tarl and I would not beg and would not die. Instead I listened as the sailors talked and I learned what was happening in the city. Ottmar had made himself king. Company, Great Company, over the seas, had fallen and no ships came any more, and Ottmar had learned of it first and moved in the night. His Whips took those he called his enemies as they slept, all the Families, all the Houses, the men, the women, the children too, and gave them no trial and no choice, but threw them off the cliff in the dawn. All of them, while Ottmar watched. The sailors said they came down screaming like gulls and as heavy as sacks of wheat in the hold of a ship, and lay broken on the rocks, waiting for the tide to wash them away. House Chandler, House Kruger, House Bowles, House Sinclair and all the rest. The sailors laughed at it. Nobody loved the Houses, they were glad to see them go. Except, I heard the sailors say, one was saved, from House Bowles, a girl called Pearl, who was the most beautiful, and she would be Ottmar's new queen.

Tarl looked at Pearl: 'They didn't know you'd run away. Ottmar must have hidden it. No one runs from marrying a king.'

Pearl sank her face deeper in her hands. Her mother dead, screaming like a seabird; her sister who thought only of pleasures, and shed tears and slapped her maid if a hem was crooked, screaming too, with her gown trailing like a wing behind her; and her father, a proud man who would never plead, falling like a swollen sack and bursting on the rocks. She thought of Hubert, with Hari's knife flashing towards him. Hubert, in a way, had been spared.

She felt Hari's eyes on her and lifted her hands. He tried to smile. She heard his silent voice comforting her, but there was no comfort.

They cut me down at nightfall, Tarl went on. They threw salt water on my back and chained me in my cell, with a pannikin of water and a heel of bread; and we sailed on, how long I don't know – there were other stops on the way and we waited there. Then we came to a port where carts rumbled and men shouted and soldiers marched on the wharf. They were leaving for the city on another ship to strengthen Ottmar's army. Whips unloaded us and packed the salt mine workers into cattle trucks and hauled them behind a steam engine up into the mountains where the mine gaped like an open mouth. Me they put in another cell, where three others waited, all of us for Deep Salt. Four days we were there, perhaps five. It was dark, I couldn't tell. They pushed food and water through a hole in the door, and we fought for it.

Tarl looked at Tealeaf: But I am Tarl and I got my share. Keeping myself strong was all I thought of. I still thought I would be able to escape. Then they brought us out into the sunlight. They shackled us and marched us along a track by the railway, and I thought: Deep Salt's up there, in the mine. But I was wrong. We turned away, following a narrower railway towards a grey hill between green hills, and came at night to a hut beside an oil lamp on a post. A sentry stood there, guarding an iron door in the base of the hill. This then, I thought, is Deep Salt. This is nothing. One sentry. I will break out of here. I hid a stone in my hand to work on my chains, but the sentry saw and only smiled.

We waited all night. In the morning a new sentry took the place of the old. It was midday before a jigger worked by two prisoners came along the line to the iron door, pulling a cart in which two ghosts sat. Ghosts, that was what I thought.

Tarl shivered. His hands moved convulsively. My mind was not my own, he said, still speaking through Tealeaf. Hunger and the sun burning down had made me weak. When I looked again I saw they were men dressed in some metal I'd never seen, like iron, but softer, and grey like the sores that scab a man dying from the sickness of the drains. They wore it like clothes; their hands were covered, and their heads, and they wore plates of glass over their eyes. They moved as if they were sick, or old and tired, from the weight they carried on their bodies. There was a clerk with them, an Ottmar clerk with the Ottmar emblem. He waited at the door for the ghosts to come. One of those men, the grey ghosts, held a little box made of the same grey metal. The other had a bolt gun, fully charged.

The clerk took a key from his belt and one from the sentry and opened the iron door. A puff came out like gas from a broken grave, and he cried at the Whips to be quick. They reached inside, into the dark, and pulled out a cart running on rails that led away. They put water on it in a barrel, and food in a sack, and left enough room for the ghosts to sit. Then they chained us behind, the four of us, and pushed the cart into the tunnel and closed the door. It made a sound like – Hari (he looked at his son), it was like the great lid that falls when they lock slaves in the hold of

154

an iron ship. And yet I thought: Wait. Wait and see. I will break out of here.

The cart began to move. It was on a pulley. A rope ran behind it and in front. Somewhere in the hill men were pulling us towards them. There was no light. But I was first in line, and I stepped up and rode on the cart without the ghosts knowing, and I listened to them. Their voices boomed inside the metal pots on their heads and echoed in mine. So I learned what Ottmar planned to do.

The ghost with the box said: We must be quick. I don't trust these suits, I don't trust the gloves, and the glass doesn't keep it out. I'll take a handful. Only one. And get it in the box, then out of here.

The other, the one with the bolt gun, said: What will he do with it, Ottmar, the king?

Learn it. Study it, the other said. And when he knows, we'll take it into the burrows and open the box and the light will come out and burn the vermin in their hiding places. They'll sicken and die and our city will be clean. Then Ottmar will go into the plains and use it to kill the rebels. And into the jungles to clear out the savages who live there. And one day, when he knows it better and knows the weapons it will make, we'll sail over the seas and conquer the old lands and rule there. We have a glorious future. But . . .

The other waited.

We must be in and out of here without a breath. I'll be quick and you be watchful. Shoot any man who comes close.

So I knew, Tarl said, what Ottmar planned. But I didn't know what this thing was they would hide in the box. I rode and waited. I would seize the bolt gun when I had seen. I would kill the ghosts. I would lead the slaves of Deep Salt out into the sunlight and kill the sentry and kill the clerk and steal a ship and sail to the city and arm the burrows and use this weapon, whatever it was, against Ottmar. That was my plan. I made it in an instant.

Tarl paused. He had seemed to swell. Now he shrank again. His head dipped closer to the table, and his voice, Tealeaf speaking with his tones and accent, sank to a whisper:

And an instant later it was gone.

He looked up. His eyes were lifeless.

The darkness faded, he said. Light grew in the tunnel ahead of us, a green light, the colour of decay, and it touched my skin the way the stealth-fly lands in the night, with a touch you don't feel, and lays its eggs under your skin. I felt the prickle of it, but only when it was done, and felt the eggs hatch, and felt the light wriggling into me, and I knew then that Deep Salt was beyond anything I had ever imagined. I said to myself: I am dead.

He turned to Hari.

Hari, my son, I spoke those words. I am dead.

Tealeaf stopped. Gantok said nothing. Pearl sat motionless on her stool, with her face whiter than mountain snow. Then Tarl laid his head on the table and wept. No one moved until Hari, holding out his hands like a father to a sick child, stepped forward and laid his arm across Tarl's back and put his head beside Tarl's on the table and waited until his sobbing stopped.

'We came for you, Tarl. You're alive,' he said.

'Yes, you came,' Tarl said in a muffled voice. 'But I'm not Tarl any more. I'm Tarl who was burned. I'm Tarl who died.'

You're Tarl who has seen evil, Tealeaf said. And felt it too, on your skin. But you didn't die like the others from Deep Salt. You've seen the horror that wriggles like worms, and wriggles like a worm in the minds of men, and you've come back and told us what you'll do – go into the burrows and lead your people away from whatever it is these ghosts carry in their box. But Tarl, you haven't told us yet what you saw in Deep Salt when you came to the place where the light has its source. Tell us that. End your story, and let us decide what we can do.'

Tarl raised his head and looked at her. He wiped his wet face on his sleeve.

'Some water,' he said hoarsely.

Hari stood and poured him a glass from a jug on a side-table. Tarl drank, then ran the last inch into his palm and splashed it on his forehead and cheeks. 'My skin still has the filth on it,' he said. 'I'll never be free.'

'You are free, Tarl. Freer than before,' Tealeaf said.

'Woman, you don't know. But I'll go on, and in my own voice. More water, Hari.' He drank again.

'I clung to the cart as the light grew brighter. We came to a cavern lit up as though the sun shone inside, but it was green, and it was a sun shining from everywhere. I could hardly see. My eyes burned. But I made out men, a band of them, ten or fifteen, with their skins burned white, waiting at the place where the rails stopped. Some of them pulled on a rope that doubled back between the lines. They stopped the cart and the ghosts got off, and the one with the bolt gun kept the men back until both of them were standing free. The men, the shrivelled wretches, the dead, Hari, the dead – for they were that and must have known it – crowded round the cart and lifted the sack down, and the barrel, and one screamed: "There's not enough." The ghost with the gun boomed at them: "The cart will come back with another load when we're out of here." He counted them and found three missing – three gone into the caves that opened at the sides of the cavern, gone to the rats that lived there. "We've brought four new workers," he said. "See that they get their share." He laughed – a sound that echoed on the ceiling and walls. He unshackled us.'

'What was the other ghost doing?' Gantok said.

'I'm coming to it. At the other end of the cavern was a mound of earth like the silt that washes out from drains after a storm and dries in the sun, and it was there the men must dig, for there were wooden spades and rakes at the foot of it. A wide vein, half as wide as the cavern, went into the hill. It was yellow, this earth, and yet it hid green inside it.'

'Made of what?' Gantok said.

'Salt, old man. Deep salt.'

'And what is that?'

'I don't know. But I know men die of it.'

'So what was the other ghost doing?'

'He raised a trapdoor in the floor of the cavern and green light struck out, and I saw all the bones in his body like a tree. He reached into the hole, deep down, and drew out his hand, dripping fire, green fire. He dropped what he held into the box and closed the lid, then closed the trapdoor. The light, the worst of it, went out.'

'What was in the hole?'

'I never saw. How long was I there?'

'Two days, perhaps. No more, or you wouldn't have fought your way back from the sickness,' Tealeaf said.

'Two days. And I saw no grain of the green salt found. That's how rare it is, even though it makes the yellow earth shine with its light. The workers call it Bad Stuff, that's all. When they find a grain – no larger than a piece torn off the end of your fingernail – they run to the hole in the floor and drop it in and close the lid and try to forget. That's all. But if they can show the ghosts who bring the food that there's a new burn mark on a spade, they get extra food. That's how it works. That is Deep Salt.'

Tarl cupped his hand. 'The ghost took that much and closed the box. He and his escort climbed on the cart and told the men, the slaves, the dead, to pull hard on the rope or there would be no more food that day, so they pulled and the cart rolled away and was gone. And I was in Deep Salt and I was dead. I knew it, Hari.'

'Until you heard my voice,' Hari said.

'Yes. It came like a thought. It came like a whisper. It came like the wind, Hari, blowing on my face. It said: Follow me, and I followed, and you know the rest. A dead man came walking in the caves.'

'You're not dead. You fought the rats. Without you we wouldn't have got out.'

'And now . . .' Tarl stopped, and Tealeaf put her hand forward and touched her fingers on the back of his. He drew away.

'I need no more help,' he said. 'I only need my son.'

'What for, Tarl?'

'To go back to the city. To rouse the burrows. To lead the people, tell them of the danger of the salt, and find it and destroy it. To fight Ottmar.'

'The salt can't be destroyed,' Tealeaf said.

'You don't know.'

'It must be stolen. And carried back into the hill where it was found and put there, in its place, and then the hill must be locked forever.'

No one spoke for a moment. Into the hill again: Hari felt sick.

Then Tarl cried, 'Who will do that?'

Again no one spoke. No one spoke aloud. But Pearl, not moving on her stool, not moving even her eyes, said to Hari in a voice not even Tealeaf heard: I'll go, Hari. I'll steal it and put it back. Will you come with me?

Hari answered: Yes, I'll come.

ELEVEN

The little boat was heavily laden. Tarl sat in the bow, staring ahead, with Dog leaning against his thigh. He brooded, he watched, and never spoke. Pearl and Hari sat in the stern with the tiller between them, Pearl ready to jump up and trim the sail or balance the sacks of food and skins of water if the wind shifted. She kept an anxious eye on the horizon, looking for storms. A big wind might swamp the small craft.

Tealeaf knew their plan, there was no hiding it from her.

I'm coming too, she had said.

No, Tealeaf, Pearl said. Three's too many. Hari knows the burrows and I know City. We can go secretly. No one will find us. And we know what you've taught us – we know it now. How to make men not see. How to make them forget.

Does Tarl know what you plan to do?

Hari's told him. Tarl doesn't think we can find the box. He thinks we – he thinks Hari will die. But he knows we have to try or the burrows will be poisoned. He'll go there, to Blood Burrow, and tell his people.

And save them from this Keech, Tealeaf said. And make them ready to fight.

Fight Ottmar. That's what he says. But I don't know what goes on in his mind. He thinks he's losing his son.

They landed on a beach at midday and ate and rested, then sailed on. The same the next day, and still Tarl sat in the bow and never spoke. They went far out to sea, passing the three hills and Saltport. Tarl turned his eyes away from them and clenched his hands in Dog's fur until he yelped.

'Tarl,' Hari said, 'we're past. It's behind us.'

They sailed four more days, sleeping in hidden inlets in the night; and saw the city mansions on the clifftops, blinking their windows in the dawn light, on the fifth. They sat far out at sea all day, waiting for dark. The brown cliffs and white houses drew back into the shade. Over beyond Port, the dark stain of the burrows went on and on, climbing into the ruined land. Plumes of smoke went up, bending in the wind.

The burrows are burning, Hari said.

The city's burning, Pearl replied. She thought of the woman, Tilly, and hoped she and her baby, born by now perhaps, were safe in their house by the city wall.

We should have painted our sail black, Hari said.

In the dark hour before the moon came up they sailed past moored empty ships, making no sound, and between two deserted wharves. Pearl lowered the sail, and together she and Hari unshipped the mast and laid it flat. They pulled the boat under the nearer wharf, into the piles, and tied it there.

'Tarl,' Hari said, and at last his father stirred.

'Hari, when you have the box, bring it to me. I'll never open it, I promise you. But I'll use it to bargain with Ottmar. That will be my weapon. Don't take it back into the hill. Bring it to me.' But he spoke with only half himself, and Hari knew he did not believe he and Pearl would succeed. They were going to their deaths.

He thought: Dead or not, I've lost my father. I'll never let

161

him have the box. No one will have it. We'll put this poison back under the hill where it belongs.

A deep grief for his father filled him, and for himself. He bowed his head at Tarl and lied: 'Yes, Tarl. I'll do as you say.'

They took supplies of water and food and climbed through the piles, with Dog swimming below. Hidden in the shadows of buildings at the base of the wharf, they paused and listened. No movement. No sound except, far away, in the city, a single hollow boom from a bolt gun.

'Where will you go, Tarl?'

'To Blood Burrow.' He touched Hari on the shoulder. 'Find me there.'

'I'll find you.' He meant it. When the box was safely in the caves, he would come back for Tarl. 'Be careful, Tarl. Keech is cunning. He's quick.'

'I'll make a pact with him. We'll fight together until Ottmar's dead.'

What then? Hari thought.

Tarl spoke no word to Pearl. 'Come with me, Dog.' He slipped away around the side of the building. Dog ran after him without a backward glance.

The only way Tarl knows is to fight, Hari said.

He hates me because I'm Company, Pearl said.

We're nothing now. You're not Company and I'm not Blood Burrow.

They put their packs of food and water on their backs and crept through silent streets into Port. There had been looting and scavenging. There had been murder too. They passed bodies that the dog packs and the rats had not found yet. There must be plenty of food for them elsewhere, plenty of corpses. Hari led cautiously. He did not know Port except for the water world under the wharves. It had been too dangerous to risk thieving in the streets – too many Whips on

162

patrol. Now they were gone, but the silence and the stillness, the black doorways and down-slanting steps and hollow windows, seemed even more threatening.

Where are we going? Pearl said.

A street where I can get my bearings. Once there I'll know the way to go.

They came to the place where Port joined Bawdhouse Burrow, where women had sold themselves to sailors at the boundary wall, and passed into the no-man's land between. Hari found an alleyway he knew and in a moment stood at the door of Lo's cell.

Lo lived here. He taught me how to speak with rats and dogs.

And horses, Pearl said, remembering Hubert tossed from his mount.

I taught myself horses. Lo taught me Company and the wars.

He pulled the curtain back. A ray of light from the newly risen moon struck through the window of the cell. The old man's skeleton gleamed dully on the floor – a crushed skull, criss-crossed bones, that was all. The dogs had been thorough.

They were starving, Hari thought. Lo wouldn't have minded. And better the dogs than the rats.

He let the curtain fall. Lo seemed far away. Lo was gone.

Stay close to me, Pearl. And feel with your mind. Make sure no one follows. I'll feel out the way in front.

She let him lead. He was the one who knew. Her turn would come if they had to go into the city.

They passed through Keg Burrow. There was no life in the streets and none in the ruins, but signs of fighting were everywhere.

Keech and Keg fought here. The women from Bawdhouse

163

too. See that body. She's still holding her knife, Hari said.

But she's only a child.

You grow up quickly in the burrows. Keech won this fight. Keg must be dead. And the women who led the Bawdhouse. The ones who survived will be in Keech's army now.

Where will he be?

In Keech Burrow. But he'll have his scouts out. We'll have to be careful.

They heard shrieks from far away and close at hand, heard moaning in doorways and, once, down a long street, saw a red fire with black figures dancing in front of it.

Where's Blood Burrow?

On the far side of Keech. Tarl will try to unite them. But he'll have to do it quickly.

They went over rubble stacks and crawled through archways, and slithered in drains under open places that had been wide streets.

Now we're in Blood Burrow, Hari said.

I hear dogs.

They're in People's Square.

He slid through a broken wall into a building, climbed a fractured beam to higher rooms and ran towards the distant sound. Soon he reached the hall with the mosaic floor where he had crawled to safety on the day Tarl had been taken. Pearl came panting behind.

Aren't we going away from the city? she said.

I want to see what's happening to Tarl.

He ran through the hall and climbed slanting floors and crushed furniture, passed the hole in the floor of East Gate, and went round the square until he came to the window where, on that day that seemed so long ago, he had lain and watched Whips chain Tarl to a cart and march him away.

He lay down and peered through the hole, then broke

164

away rotten wood for Pearl as she lay beside him.

There was no sound of dogs now but the stink of a dog pack filled the air. Hari did not see it at first – saw instead the swamp, with Cowl the Liberator raising his green head from the water and holding his blunt sword high. Then he saw the dogs below him, and saw Tarl.

It was the dog pack Hari had stolen the black and yellow dog from – the dog called Dog. The pack was stronger now, doubled in number, but the old grey-muzzled hound still led. And Hari saw at once that Dog had challenged it. The two stood in an open space, the leader in front of his pack and Dog opposite him, with Tarl a dozen steps behind. Tarl would not interfere, not openly. This was a leaders' fight.

They circled each other, growling, and Hari thought: Dog will lose. Then they'll kill Tarl.

The leader was a tall hound, tough in his body, strong in his head, long jawed and scarred from many fights. Yet he showed some uncertainty as the smaller dog circled him with its lip curled back. Dog was not the sick animal Hari had ordered to follow him. His limp was gone. Rest in the village, good food, plenty of food, had made him strong. He had grown thick chested, his wide flat head seemed bonier, and his mouth had sharp back-slanting teeth and thicker ones deep in the angle of his jaw. He trembled with pent-up strength and energy.

The moment of attack was too fast to see. It was Dog who moved, going not for the leader's throat, as Hari had expected, but for one of his front legs, snapping it with a single bite . . .

Hari said: Tarl's helping him. I hear Tarl's voice.

Pearl drew back from the window. She closed her eyes and put her fingers in her ears. Hari did not blame her. He wanted to do the same.

165

Now his throat, Tarl's voice said, and Dog obeyed, and almost as quickly as it had started the fight was over.

Dog tightened his grip, jerked, tore, then stepped back and howled his triumph. Tarl stood without moving. The dog pack rushed forward and ripped at the leader's body until there were only scraps of hair and broken bones left.

It's over, Pearl.

Can we go?

There are people coming.

They crept from holes and doorways round People's Square.

Tarl waited. Again Hari heard his voice speaking to Dog: Bring your dogs behind you. Tell them there'll be food. Make them know I'm your friend.

Dog gave three short barks, and the animals slunk past him and clustered behind. He strutted back and forth in front of them. Hari could not hear what he said.

The people crept closer. They carried knives and spears and spikes of broken wood and clubs made of iron and stone.

Tarl broke through the pack and stood beside Dog. He faced the thickening crowd and stopped their progress by raising his hand.

'I am Tarl,' he said. 'I have come back from Deep Salt.'

A hiss ran through the crowd, a deepening whisper, neither of belief nor disbelief, until a woman's voice at the back cried: 'No one comes back from Deep Salt.'

'I am Tarl. Tarl comes back. Look at me. Here is my right arm. Here is my knife.' He pushed hair back from his forehead. 'And here is the mark Company burned on me when I was taken.'

'No one comes back. You have stolen his shape.'

'You have devoured him.'

166

'You have eaten his soul.'

'You are not Tarl.'

They'll kill him, Pearl whispered.

No. My father is changed.

Tarl singled out a man, a thickset fellow with a bulging face, and said, 'Trabert, I hear your voice. Have you made yourself leader of Blood Burrow? Would you like to fight me the way the dogs fought?'

'No one leads. And no one fights with a ghost.'

Tarl smiled. He raised his knife and ran the tip along the angle of his jaw. Blood dripped on his chest.

'Do ghosts bleed?'

Again the crowd hissed, while the dogs whined at the smell of blood.

A woman cried, 'If you're Tarl and not dead, does your son Hari live too?'

'He drowned,' cried another. 'We saw him drown in the swamp. Over by the wall.'

'No,' Tarl cried. 'He swam. He found a hole in the wall and came up on the other side. Hari lives. Hari can move in the shadows. Hari can pass without being seen. He has gone to steal the weapon Ottmar found in Deep Salt. A weapon that burns men into dust. He will bring it to me, and we will fight Ottmar and turn him into dust.'

He spoke silently to Dog: Make your pack howl.

Dog raised his muzzle and gave a looping cry, and the whole pack followed – a sound that made Pearl and Hari shrink back from the window. When it had died, Tarl cried, 'The dogs know. They'll follow me. Do you follow me too?'

'Men don't run with dogs,' Trabert said, although his eyes darted fearfully.

'The times have changed. And men – the men of Blood Burrow – must change with them. Company is gone, but not gone. Company is called Ottmar now, and he is worse. He plans to kill us all with his weapon. So we must join with Keech and we must wait. You, Trabert, you, Wonk, you have acted wisely. You have let Ottmar and the clerk army fight, and the workers too. They fight each other. But we mustn't copy them and fight with Keech. We must join him and wait and be ready. When they have exhausted each other, then we strike. The burrows strike. We will fight in our way – from doorways, from holes in the ground. Strike and be gone. We will be shadows. Shadows with knives, too fast for their bolt guns. They'll never see us. And we will have Ottmar's weapon too, when Hari brings it. When it is done, the city will be ours again, and its name will be Belong, the way it was before Company came.'

'And will Blood Burrow rule or will Keech?' Trabert said.

'That is a matter for another day. I'll see to Keech. But now, on this day, will you follow me?'

They will, Hari said. They'll follow him.

He drew back from the window.

Come on, Pearl. He stood up and took her hand and pulled her to her feet. Let's find Ottmar's box and take it back to the dead hill before someone opens it and kills the city and the world.

TWELVE

They spent the night and the next day in the room where Tarl had kept his weapons and food, knowing he would be too busy at People's Square to come this far.

At nightfall they made their way along the foot of the city wall. A stormwater drain ran out and dropped into a ditch winding to the sea. In the days of Company there had been guards to stop burrows men from creeping in. Now it stood unguarded, a black hole in the fitted blocks of stone.

I could never get in here, but I came down once from Compound, to learn the way in case I had to run, Hari said.

Where will we come out?

Beside the house with the flag that has the yellow flame. House Sinclair.

The rats are small. They won't get in our way.

I'm not frightened of rats, Hari. I'm not frightened of anything now.

Let's get into the dark before the moon comes up.

The drain was tall enough for them to walk upright. It ran with no more than an inch of water. Smaller inlets came from the sides and several from the roof, dripping moisture. They followed the main drain until they were under the city. Hari stopped at a side drain.

Now we crawl – and hope it doesn't rain or we'll get washed out. He dowsed the torch he had lit at the entrance. We climb by touch.

The sides were slippery. They had to brace themselves with knees and forearms to move up. In the steep places they used iron handholds fixed in the wall. Both climbed easily, hardened by their long walk through the mountains and jungle and their sailing of the boat. But Hari felt a growing unease in Pearl's mind as they climbed towards the place where she had lived. Her resolve, though, was equal to his. He had seen the green light, the misshapen rats, and he meant to take the poison salt that created them back into the dark where it belonged. She meant to take it from the man who had killed her family and stop him from killing anyone else.

Light leaked into the drain from higher up.

We're nearly at the street. The moon's out. There's no sump, just an opening at the kerb. We'll have to take our packs off to get through.

He peered out and sent his mind questing.

No one's guarding here. The houses look empty.

They'll be up at the other end, Pearl said. At House Ottmar and Kruger and Bowles.

There's only one sentry on the walls. He must have taken every spare man for his army.

Hari took off his pack and pushed it onto the road. He slid through the opening at the kerb. Pearl followed.

Dogs are howling down there, she said. Is that the burrows?

Tarl's pack. He must be meeting Keech.

The sentry was listening to the noise, with his back to the

street. Pearl and Hari ran across; and now, in the place where she had lived all her life, Pearl led – although, Hari thought, I know it as well as her. I've spied out every hiding place along the cliffs.

They climbed the fence to House Sinclair, where the lawn grass, uncut, tangled their feet and the clipped shrubs had sprouted at their tops. Litter strewed the paths and flowerbeds. The house must have been used for barracks before Ottmar sent his troops into the city to fight.

Pearl and Hari crept around to the back. They sent their minds probing for hidden watchers. None. House Parlane and House Bassett lay ahead, with their wide parks running to the cliff edge. Both were deserted. Next came House Bowles. Pearl lifted herself and looked over the wall.

There are soldiers there.

It's another barracks.

Exhausted men lay sleeping on the lawns or resting against the walls with their heads drooping.

They've been in a battle, Pearl said. The house must be full. I'm glad I don't have to go inside.

There's a path along the cliff. We'll use that.

They ran through the gardens of House Bassett, crouching at low places in the wall separating it from House Bowles. They climbed the far end and were hidden from the mansion by hedges, growing ragged, and ornamental trees losing shape. A wrought-iron fence cut the path off from the edge of the cliff. Pearl stopped at a bench placed to give a view out to sea and along the coast.

I want to sit down a moment, Hari.

She had come here with Tealeaf on fine evenings and also in the night when House Bowles was sleeping, and Tealeaf had taught her the names of the stars and told her how the moon controlled the tides and why the winds blew and

171

many more things. They had watched the busy port, with its streets marked out by gas lamps, and the ships tied up at the wharves, loading grain and coal and tea and timber – and salt, she remembered with a shudder. Now the port was dark, not a light to be seen, except for the dying glow of a warehouse burned by looters.

In the other direction, the cliff advanced jaggedly into the sea. She had not looked that way, and Tealeaf had not told her the stories, but she had heard them anyway, in children's talk, and knew that where the park between House Bowles and House Ottmar ran down to the cliff, and was clenched like a fist over the black reef far below, the Families had been murdered in the old days, before Company made its great conquest in the War. Tealeaf had, in the end, told her that. It explained the monument raised there – a white marble hand, the Company hand, set on a plinth, with its fingers hooked in agony or revenge.

Pearl sat on the bench. Hari sat beside her and waited. She looked across the park at the hand (while Hari remembered that he had always spat on it in passing) and the jutting rock beyond. Ottmar was using the rock to murder people again. She remembered her family, found good things to remember, and tears began to trickle on her face.

Blossom, she thought. Blossom used to dress me in her old dresses when I was small. She brushed my hair and tied ribbons in it. Blossom really should have been a maid. That would have made her happy. And Hubert loved horses better than people. Hubert should have been a groom. She could not think of anything her father should have been, or her mother, or William and George, but she cried for them all the same. After a while she dried her eyes and stood up.

I'm finished now.

It's a quick way to die, Hari said.

Be quiet, Hari.

They crossed the park, leaving the cliff behind. The wall cutting off House Ottmar was higher than the one between House Bowles and the park. Pearl climbed on Hari's shoulders and hauled herself up.

There's no one here, but the house is lit up.

She reached down and Hari jumped for her hand and climbed to the top.

There's no sound of fighting in the city. Ottmar must have come back. There'll be guards on the house.

But none in the gardens. They think there's no danger from out here.

The mansion was lit only on the ground floor. Pearl and Hari jumped down and ran, then paused and crept, feeling for anyone who might be hidden behind the hedges or in the flowering trees. They waited while a new sentry took the place of the one at the back door. The off-duty soldier walked to a fountain on the lawn, where he splashed water on his face and drank from his cupped hands.

They're soldiers, not Whips, Pearl said.

Bolt guns, not gloves, Hari said.

I'll take the one at the door. You get the one on the corner.

He shrugged, then smiled. He had grown up with women who kept quiet until they were asked. Everything was changing. He found he did not mind.

Pearl crawled as far as the fountain, where light from the windows began to reach. She glimpsed Hari behind the hedge at the corner of the house; felt his mind go out and immobilise the sentry. She stood up and walked towards the man at the door. He straightened, half cried out – she had appeared like a ghost – then swung his bolt rifle down from his shoulder. But she was close enough: Be still, she said,

173

just as she had heard Tealeaf say it on the night they had escaped.

Mouth open, rifle pointed above her head, he obeyed, although she felt his mutinous lurch before she had him in control. She was going to have to get better at this. She walked up to him, soft on the grass.

Put up your rifle. Stand in your place.

He obeyed.

Hari? she called.

Yes, I've got him. Easy.

She doubted that.

Come on then, before there's anyone else.

He ran back into the dark, avoiding the lighted windows, then came across the lawn from behind the fountain.

Pearl said to the sentry: No one has been here. You've seen no one. She pushed the whole of her mind into the command and saw his eyes deaden.

Ask him, Hari began.

Quiet, Hari. She knew what to say.

Where is Ottmar?

'In the war room with his commanders,' the man said woodenly.

Where's Kyle-Ott?

'With them.'

Are there guards in the house?

'Outside the war room. And at the front door and the gate.'

And where does Ottmar keep the salt?

She nearly lost him then. He gave a start, his eyes showed a gleam of consciousness, and Hari, behind her, said: Be still.

It's a narrow path, he whispered to Pearl. We've got to hold them on it and not let them step off.

Yes. She reinforced Hari's command: Be still. Then said:

174

Ottmar has a new weapon. Where does he keep it?

The sentry seemed to think, and she felt memories circling like slow fish in his mind. He said: 'Men came with a box.'

How long ago?

'Six days.'

Where did they take it?

'Into the basement where the servants sleep.'

Which end? The women's or the men's?

'The women's end.'

Are they still there?

'They haven't come out.'

Then stand at your post. Forget you've seen us. When we're gone we were never here.

They slipped through the open door into the back entrance hall. Pearl had been to banquets and balls in the Ottmar mansion where, only recently, she had caught Ottmar's eye, and Kyle-Ott's as well, but she had never been in this part of the house. The great rooms lay ahead – the reception room, the dining room, the ballroom, the galleries, while the living rooms and bedrooms were upstairs – but off this back entrance were only kitchens and sculleries. The war room, Pearl guessed, was the former ballroom. Ottmar would choose the grandest space for making his plans.

Stairs to the basement led down on either side. Pearl did not know which ones went to the women's dormitory, but caught a female smell, female sweat, from the left and turned that way. They went cautiously down unlit steps, feeling their way. At the bottom was the room where the women servants ate their food. Tables and chairs were pushed against the walls to make room for wooden beds thrown in as though for a bonfire. The dormitory must have been cleared to make way for the men working on the salt.

They went through the room, opened a door quietly on

the far side and peered along a corridor lit by a lamp at the end. A guard stood halfway along, with his head in shadow and his feet in a sheet of light coming under a door.

There's another corridor going off, Hari said, so there must be a back way in.

He slipped out of the room and was swallowed in a black cave. Pearl followed.

They found themselves in a narrower corridor. Dimly, at the end, light spread from under another door. Walking softly, nervous of creaking boards, they went to it and felt for people on the other side.

Two men. Along at the far end, Pearl said.

They're afraid. Feel their fear. The salt is there.

How do you know?

I've been close to it. But there's no light. They must be keeping the box closed.

He turned the handle of the door, holding it firmly so it wouldn't squeak.

Stop a minute, Hari, Pearl said. I'll make them look the other way.

How?

Tealeaf taught me while you were with Danatok finding Tarl.

She sent out soft commands, making them like puffs of breeze through a field of grass, bending the stalks and making the seed heads sway: See where the wind travels. See where it goes.

Now they're looking away.

Watching the grass. You'll have to teach me that one day, Hari said.

Open the door. Do it quietly.

They slipped through, and Hari closed it behind him.

This room was bigger than the eating room. Along one

wall at the near end was a long table with water buckets on it for washing. Latrine cubicles with open doors lined the opposite wall. Further off, more wooden beds lay in a heap, hiding the far end of the room where two gas lamps glowed in the ceiling.

They heard the sound of heavy boots on a wooden floor. Then voices came, booming as though in a hollow place.

'How many?'

'One hundred.'

'We'll have to fill them slowly. Only three or four a night. It's too dangerous otherwise.'

'He wants them now.'

'We'll tell him . . .'

The other voice interrupted: 'Tell him what? Do you tell Ottmar? Do I?'

'But Slade, the radiation's coming through. It's coming through the lead, through the suits. We're both sick. It's killing us.'

'Ottmar is killing us.'

'We've got to get out of here.' The man began to cry, weak voiced, like a sick child.

'Shut up, Coney,' said the other.

Crouching, moving carefully, Pearl and Hari hid behind the pile of beds and looked through a lattice-work of snapped and twisted legs. Two men in suits of grey metal – the lead they spoke of, Hari supposed – stood under the lamps. In front of them on a table lay a small flat box made of the same grey metal.

Is that it? Pearl said.

Must be.

It's not even as big as my jewel box. What if they open the lid?

They won't, it's sealed. Anyway, they're frightened. Pearl,

177

we need to get it out of here quick, and back in Deep Salt. You heard them, they're sick with it even inside those suits they're wearing.

I'll take the far one, you take the near. Hold them hard. But what do we do then?

We grab the box and run.

Is that all?

Can you think of anything better? If we can get into the drain, we're safe. Are you ready?

Wait. Wait.

She put her hand on his arm, keeping him still, and heard again the sound that had alerted her.

Footsteps, Hari said.

Someone's coming.

If they use the door behind us, we're caught.

The footsteps came closer and Hari sighed. They've passed the small corridor, Pearl said. They're stopping by the guard.

They heard him stamp his feet, coming to attention. The door was thrust open and a man in the uniform of an Ottmar Whip burst in, swinging a bolt rifle to cover the room.

'Safe,' he called.

A second man, more senior, came in and pushed him aside.

'King Ottmar. The Lord Kyle-Ott,' he cried.

The men at the table had turned, slow and heavy in their metal suits. They tried to come to attention. More feet sounded in the corridor.

Ottmar came through the door and Pearl almost gave a cry at the sight of him. He was a big man, he almost filled the doorway. She had not remembered him so swollen and so broad, but perhaps his new importance inflated him: King Ottmar. He had dined in the war room and his face shone red from food and wine – as she had seen it across the table only a few months before, at a dinner in the Bowles house, arranged by Pearl's father to bring Ottmar's courtship to a head. He had seemed to take no notice of her, had been more interested in his meat, in snapping his fingers to have his wine glass filled, but every now and then she had felt his eyes settle on her face and had known this man would use her for a while, to further his importance, and for his pleasure, then throw her away. And she had felt him sip her fear as though it were wine, and seen him gulp from the glass and swill the liquid in his mouth, and heard the greedy sound as he swallowed. If it had not been for Tealeaf, by the wall with the personal maids, Tealeaf telling her to be calm, she would have jumped up and run from the table.

Now he was with her in the room again, less than a dozen steps away. His shaved head gleamed, yellow-white. The weight seemed to have slipped from it into his cheeks and jowls, leaving the skull fragile, but rolls of fat melted over each other on his neck. The uniform he wore, velvet and silk adorned with brocade and newly minted medals, shone with rainbow colours, blue and yellow and red. An odour of sweat advanced with him into the dormitory, not hidden by the perfumes he wore – the smell, Pearl thought, of lust to rule, lust to crush everything and raise it again in his image.

Kyle-Ott came behind him, and stopped a pace in the rear. But he had the same lust. It was in his eyes, restless, pushing everything back and making it small. She saw how the fire had marked him: a livid scar curved like a knife blade on his cheek.

Hari?

Don't even breathe.

He felt Ottmar's threat – felt that the man could sense something not right in the room; could smell something, perhaps. His eyes – small, set deep, taking an intensity from the darkness hiding them – saw into every corner and seemed to wind through the tangle of beds to Hari's face. He closed his own eyes slowly, so no gleam or movement would catch Ottmar's attention.

The man turned away. 'This room must be cleared. See to it in the morning.'

'Sir,' said the chief Whip.

'And put two guards on the door, not one. Now –' he turned to Slade and Coney – 'you are ready?'

'Ready, my Lord,' one of the lead-suited men replied.

'Show me.' He stepped to the table. 'The salt is there?' – indicating the box.

'Yes, Lord. Locked inside.'

'There's enough?'

'Enough for a thousand bullets if you need them, with a grain of salt locked in each. But Lord Ottmar, Majesty . . .'

'Where are the bullets?'

The man stepped ponderously to the table. 'Here, Lord.'

The objects ranked on the surface looked like mice. Hari and Pearl could not see what they were.

'How many?' Ottmar said.

'One hundred.'

'Enough. Have them loaded by morning.'

'Lord . . .'

'By morning. If they're not ready I'll have you stripped out of your suits and see if that makes you work any faster.'

'Father,' Kyle-Ott said, 'one must be saved. When I find the girl, Radiant Pearl, I'll lock her in a dark room and make her open it. Then she will burn the way she burned me.'

Pearl felt his hatred. It found her through the broken bed legs. She went deeper into herself, where he could not reach her; and, safe there, saw that hatred bent him into a creature

180

locked inside itself, with no way out. She saw it made him powerless, and she pitied him.

'You can do what you like with the girl,' Ottmar said. 'But stay behind me, remember your place.' He turned to Slade and Coney. 'At dawn,' he said.

The Whips stepped back and Ottmar strode out of the room. Kyle-Ott hurried after him. The door slammed and footsteps marched back down the corridor.

'We are dead men,' whispered Coney.

'Tomorrow he will pay us. Then I'll eat and drink and buy myself a woman. Do the same,' Slade said.

'We are dead.'

'The dead will play. Now, Coney, work.' He picked up the box.

'No,' Coney cried, 'leave the seal. Open the bullets.'

Pearl put her hand on Hari's arm. Now, she said.

Hit them hard, Pearl. These metal suits might keep us out the way they keep out the salt.

They rose to their feet and walked quietly to the men, who stood with their backs turned at the far end of the table.

Slade, Pearl said, making Hari pause. He had meant to take Slade.

Coney, he said, using all his strength, pushing it like a spear through the lead helmet deep into the man's head.

Turn and face me, Slade, Pearl said.

Turn, Coney, Hari said.

The men turned slowly. Their eyes looked out dully through the glass plates in the helmets.

Tell me, Hari said, what are these things on the table?

'Bullets,' Coney said in a thick voice.

What are they for? Pearl said.

'To shoot into the city and kill the rebel army,' Slade said.

Tell us how, Hari said, holding Coney still and joining Pearl inside Slade's mind. He picked up one of the objects from the table. It was not bullet shaped but was a ball made of the grey metal, lead.

'It's hinged on one side. It opens out,' Slade said.

Hari understood. And inside there's a hollow for a grain of Deep Salt? One grain?

'One is enough.'

How does Ottmar shoot it? Pearl said.

'He's built a cannon on the city wall. He'll shoot the bullets down like seeds. Each one is sealed, but they'll break open when they strike and the grain of salt will fly out. Then ...'

The light will be free in the city and everyone will die.

'That is Ottmar's plan. Then we'll go down in our suits of lead and find each grain from the light it throws, and put them in their box again.'

And he'll kill the burrows the same way? Hari said.

'Yes, the burrows. Then the rebel armies in the south.'

And himself.

'We haven't told him that. Ottmar wouldn't believe us. He believes only in Ottmar the King.'

Hari, take the box and go, Pearl said.

Wait, he said. Slade, here's what you'll do. Are the bullets empty?

'Yes, empty.'

Seal them, each one. When Ottmar sends his men in the morning, tell them there's a grain of salt inside. They won't check, they'll be afraid. They'll take them to Ottmar. When will the cannon shoot them into the city?

'At night, so Ottmar can stand on the hill and watch his salt lights come on.'

Does he know he'll kill every living thing?

'He knows, or he does not. Ottmar isn't like other men. He orders us to find a way to make the salt safe only for him.'

No one can do that.

'No one.'

The man seemed to speak with satisfaction. He and Coney were easier to control than Hari had expected. Perhaps it was because they were afraid – fear had weakened them and opened them out. Yet the man, Slade, had enough of himself left to take pleasure in the death of everyone, almost to taste everyone dying and smile at it. Hari recoiled from him. Then he thrust his mind back into the man, reducing him to a self no bigger than a rat.

I could kill him, he thought; and he felt something twist in him like the sickness in the cave when he had reached the fringes of the green light.

No, Hari, Pearl cried. That isn't why we can go inside them.

I can't stop it.

Yes you can. Hear your name. She breathed it into him: Hari, Hari. He recognised it, held it hard, settled it deep in his mind, and moved back inch by inch from the dark place he had been. Gradually the sickness slid out of him. He breathed deeply, stepping back from Slade.

Are you all right?

Pearl, there's another voice. I heard it. I nearly went there.

It's what Ottmar hears, Hari. And Kyle-Ott. But we hear the other voice, they don't. Now come on, we've got to go.

Yes, out of here. Make these men forget. I don't want to talk to them any more.

He went along the table and picked up the lead box, and its weight almost made him let it slip. It was warm, like the body of a newly killed rat. He opened his pack and pushed

183

the box inside, anxious to get it out of his hands.

Pearl spoke to Coney. Fear had weakened him so thoroughly it was like laying a child in a cot. She brought Slade back from the state Hari had left him in. She told him no one but Ottmar and his son had been in the room. Time had stopped when they left and would start again when midnight chimed on the house clock. He and Coney would close and seal the bullets, and give them to the soldiers who came in the morning. They would say that the salt box was back in its lead safe. That was all. Except – Pearl hesitated – except: Go from here, if you can, get far away, before Ottmar finds out his bullets are empty.

The men stood like plaster statues, not even moving their eyes.

Come on, Hari.

They went to the door beyond the broken beds and let themselves out without a sound. They slipped through the women's eating room and up the stairs. The sentry stood at his post outside the door. Pearl stole his consciousness, then made the other sentry at the corner watch a breeze rippling through the grass away from him. They ran for the fountain and into the dark.

The journey along the cliff edge, over the walls, through the gardens, took longer. Hari was weighed down by the box. He grunted as he ran, and could not understand why tears slid on his face and why they seemed to come from the salt, not from himself.

Pearl turned the wall sentry to face the burrows while she and Hari crossed the road and wriggled into the drain. The Ottmar clock struck midnight – a dying sound – as they dropped through the narrow wet ways. Hari wore his pack in front as they slid down inclines on their backs. In the large drain, Pearl was able to light the torch and lead at a fast unbroken pace. She dowsed it at the entrance and Hari took the lead, keeping them in the ditch that ran to the sea. In places it was lined with stone, but mostly the walls had crumbled. Hari would not have used a way so perfect for ambush except that he heard, far off, the howling of dogs, punctuated as though someone controlled it. He supposed the meeting was still taking place, and perhaps an alliance was made, in Blood Burrow or in Keech. All of the burrows would be there.

Tarl, he thought, be careful – but had no strength for more than that, because the box, holding its warmth and weight against his body, seemed to drain him in another way.

They reached the place where the ditch emptied into the sea.

Along here now, to the wharves.

Dark alleys, back ways he was unfamiliar with. He called Pearl beside him and let her feel for hidden men, hidden women too. It was almost dawn when they reached the wharf that concealed their boat. They swam through the piles and climbed inside, and Hari pulled his pack off at once. It had almost dragged him down.

I can't keep this near me, he said.

Pearl lifted it and felt its weight and its prickle of warmth.

Hari, tie a rope on it and drop it over the side. The water might keep it from hurting us.

It might make it worse.

But he tied a piece of cord to the straps, then climbed as far away as he could through the piles and lowered the pack into the water. The weight of the box dragged it down. He tied the cord to a pile strut. Swimming and climbing back, he felt cleaner.

They ate, then slept, exhausted enough not to care that

they were wet. Sun rays slanting between the wharf planks told them it was mid-afternoon when they woke.

We can't go till dark, Hari said.

Why not? There are no boats to chase us. Why chase us anyway? Won't everyone be looking into the city, waiting to see what Ottmar's cannon does?

She was right.

And we'll be out at sea before they know it's nothing. Slade and Coney won't tell. They'll be gone.

Hari was glad she was able to think. He did not seem to be able to work things out any more.

They waited a while longer, listening for sounds. Then Hari went through the piles and brought back his pack, trailing it under water all the way.

Tie it on the back of the boat, Pearl said. We can bring it up when we get to Deep Salt.

It'll drag. It'll slow us down.

But we'll be safer. It doesn't matter how long we take.

He tied the pack and let it sink. They guided the boat through the piles into open water, raised the mast and sail, and slowly, in a breeze almost too light to feel, steered away from Port and out to sea.

Sunset was golden, and the mansions on the cliffs shone white and yellow and blue. Their windows flashed, but neither Pearl nor Hari, straining their eyes, could see any movement of people. Below the city wall, the burrows were still, with only here and there a feather of smoke.

The wind grew fresh and swung round, pushing them further from land, but the little boat moved sluggishly, with the pack and heavy box acting like a sea anchor. Hari worked the sail, wanting more speed. Ottmar would start his light-show before the moon came up. And, when it failed, Hari sensed he would know who had stolen his salt, where it had gone. Ottmar had a voice that spoke to him too.

An afterglow held light in the western sky. Then it was gone as though someone had thrown a spade of earth on a fire. Night came quickly, sparkling with stars. Ottmar would not like the stars. He would want blackness as deep as he could get.

A few lights came on in the mansions, but Port and the burrows stayed dark. Then a boom sounded, rolling on the water like an iron wheel on a wooden floor.

He's started, Pearl said.

And now he knows, Hari said.

There was a pause. Then another boom.

He'll keep on going. He can't be sure until he's fired them all, Pearl said.

The bombardment went on.

Pearl counted. That's fifty.

And no lights in the sky, Hari said.

What will he do?

Kill people. Torture them.

Hari, there's no way he can know about us.

She was right – and yet he had heard the whisper of another voice.

A gout of flame rose between two mansions and a moment later the sound of an explosion reached them.

The army in the city's firing back. The clerks must have bolt cannons, Hari said.

Another flame rose, another detonation sounded.

They've hit one of the houses. It's House Kruger, Pearl said.

Ottmar's stopped his cannon.

He'll have to use his bolt cannons too, Hari said.

They'll kill each other, Pearl said. Both sides.

She steered the boat as Hari worked the sail, but could not keep her eyes from the fires sprouting on the cliff. The sound of cannons rolled continuously and a glow rose from the city – not the green of salt, but the orange of flames at work on buildings.

House Kruger burned. Then . . .

Hari, they've hit my house. They've hit House Bowles.

They'll hit them all. They must have been getting ready for this.

He thought of Tarl watching from the burrows – and knew he would wait. When both armies had fought themselves into exhaustion, Tarl would strike.

The burrows will win, Hari thought. It was what he had wanted all his life, what he had dreamed of. Now it filled him only with sadness. It made him afraid. Tarl or Keech or someone else would rule, but everything would stay the same.

House Kruger fell in a great explosion of fire and smoke. The small house beside it, House Roebuck, collapsed. House Bowles still burned. Pearl watched without being able to hold her memories still and find what her home had meant to her. It seemed she had spent all her life growing out of it, growing away – all that time since Tealeaf had come and turned it into nothing. Yet it had enclosed her, kept her warm, kept her fed – while Hari starved in Blood Burrow.

The top floor of the mansion suddenly crumbled and the lower walls opened like a red-petalled flower. A coil of smoke rolled up and vanished into the dark.

Gone. It's gone, Pearl thought. I'm not Bowles any more.

Are you all right? Hari said.

Yes, I'm all right.

They'll burn them all.

Let's get away from here, Pearl said.

188

THIRTEEN

They sailed through the night, then sheltered from rising winds in a little bay. A freshwater spring beyond the beach gave them water. Hari trapped fish in a shallow lagoon while Pearl found a tree that had edible fruit.

The wind was easier the next day and blew them along. They stayed close to the coast, watching for places where they could camp and find more food. After four days, the hills, two green, one grey, raised their humps on the coastline. Hari made a wide loop out to sea so that no one at Saltport would notice their sail, and landed north of the hills at the place where he and Danatok had stopped after rescuing Tarl.

Pearl, he said, I don't need you. I'll go in alone.

Hari, she answered, I don't need you. I'll go in alone.

He grinned at her slowly, then laughed.

She frowned in reply. Don't ever say anything like that again.

I'm sorry. And he was. The frown crease in her brow was a mark he had made. To underline his apology he said sorry again, out loud.

We should start now, she said. Get this salt inside, then get as far away as we can.

So they pushed the boat out from the beach and sailed along the shoreline of the nearer green hill. The tide was higher than when Danatok and Hari had come for Tarl. The sea on the north side of the grey hill was calm.

We'll tie up where the cave comes out. I can't swim with the box, it'll drag me under.

Cliffs beetled over them, shining like coal. Pearl steered the boat in and jibed, and Hari jumped out and looped a rope around a horn of rock, leaving plenty of slack for the falling tide. If the wind turned and waves came up, the boat would be driven onto the rocks: it was a risk they had to take. She lowered the sail while he hauled up his pack and let water leak out of it. He put his hand inside to feel the box.

It's still warm. He felt as if he had touched something alive.

Pearl took the half-burned torch from the locker and lit it from the tinder box. She thrust an unused torch into her belt. They climbed around the base of the rock hiding the cave, mounted blocks of stone and went into the jagged opening. At once they felt the touch of poisoned air, prickling yet soft.

This is why he didn't want me to come, Pearl thought.

Let's go fast.

Hari led, holding the torch, finding his way from a map unrolling like a parchment in his mind. They had not gone far when they heard a squeaking and shrieking like rusty doors. Eyes like red embers shone at them; wet grey snouts advanced to the edge of the light.

We'll make a wall in front of us and keep pushing them back.

The mutant rats roiled and boiled. Pearl and Hari rolled them back like rubbish in front of a broom.

They're hungry. They're starving. They'll start eating each other in a while, Hari said.

Soon he began walking slower and helping her less with the rats. She increased her pressure on them, although looking at them filled her with revulsion. Yet they would not have grown this way – naked, long furred, triple tailed – without the poison of the salt. They were twisted inside – and Ottmar wanted this twisting for his enemies. She felt a stronger revulsion for him than for the rats.

Hari?

I'm all right. This thing seems to weigh more and more.

We don't need to go all the way.

There's a side-cave near the light but not as close as I went last time. Danatok said there's a pool of water at the back. It goes down and down. He tried it with a stone tied on a string and it never got to the bottom. I'm going to sink the box in there.

They went on. The rats retreated, somersaulting, squealing. Hari grew weaker. The lead box seemed to swell against his back and make a hissing sound between his shoulder blades. It almost seemed to whisper his name.

Be quiet, he whispered in reply.

How far now? Pearl said.

Not far.

The map in his mind was tearing down the middle, but he sensed, like a hidden room, the side-cave not far ahead. In a moment it opened in the torchlight. A rat that had turned in rushed out squealing. Hari kicked it away, then had no more strength. He leaned against the wall and let the torch droop.

Pearl snatched it. She scattered the rats with a cry of rage.

Hari, she cried, give me the box. Take it off.

He raised his head. Pearl, he said, Pearl.

What?

If I keep it, I can use it to frighten Ottmar.

He slid down the wall and sat on the ground.

I can use it against both sides and make them stop fighting.

No, Hari.

I can –

No.

I want it, Pearl.

She saw rats creeping closer and blasted them back. She took the spare torch from her belt and lit it from Hari's.

Then she said: Stand up, Hari.

No . . .

Stand up.

She used all her strength and saw his eyes glaze in the torchlight. Slowly he stood, sliding up the wall the way he had slid down. The pack scraped, and one of the straps unhitched from his shoulder.

Take it off. Give it to me.

Pearl. His voice came from far away, winding past obstructions, dragging a weight that strove to hold it back.

Hari, I'm not going to make you. You can give it to me yourself.

Pearl? he whispered again. It seemed like a question. Slowly, like an old man, he turned side on to her. He took the second strap from his shoulder and put the pack down on the floor.

'Ha,' he panted, 'ha,' as though finishing a race.

Thank you, Hari. Now hold the torch.

She put it in his hand, then picked up the feebly guttering one he had dropped. She took both straps of the pack and lifted it.

Keep the rats back.

She went into the side-cave. It turned left, then right, ending in a back-slanting wall. A pool of water no larger than the scented bath where her maids had soaped her gleamed like oil in the torchlight. Pearl approached, half-carrying, half-dragging the pack – and felt a tingling, worming thing inside her, at her spine, forcing its way up with a hissing that began far away, at the edge of sound, then darted at her ear and said: Keep me, Pearl.

She was enraged.

Get out, she cried, and hefted the pack one-handed, and looped it with a side-footed kick into the pool. It lay on the surface, belching air for a moment, then sank, and she pictured it going down and down, among deformed creatures, two-headed fish, and settling on the bottom where Ottmar would never find it, or Tarl, or Hari. Or Pearl.

The thing that had breathed her name was gone. It was in me, it was me, she thought. She ran back through the cave.

It's gone, Hari, she cried.

She heard him sob. His mouth was open as though in grief. Yet he was standing, keeping the torch high. The rats milled and bit each other where the light grew dim.

Now let's get out of here, she said.

I can't, Hari said.

Hari. She pulled him.

I can't. I've got to find if anyone's alive.

She had not thought of that.

They won't be.

We don't know. If they are, we've got to get them out. We can't leave them here.

The thought of going further terrified Pearl. She looked at the rats, which seemed to hump their backs and grow their snouts, and she doubted her strength to hold them back much longer.

The torches won't last, she said.

Pearl, help me call them.

We don't know their names. And if they answer, they can't come to us through the dark. The rats will get them.

I want to call them, Pearl.

What shall we say?

Just, is anyone there?

So they tried, joining their voices and sending a silent cry into the darkness.

No one answered.

I'm trying to feel them, Hari said. He let his mind fly like a bat, but it flapped and circled in a green-lit cave he could only imagine, and nothing moved there, nothing breathed.

Help me, Pearl.

She tried.

Hari, they're all dead, she said.

We've got to go round and open the door so they can come out.

It was Tarl he pictured – Tarl ragged, beaten, filthy, sick, feeling his way through the poisonous light.

All right, Pearl said. The iron door. We open the door. But Hari, come on. If we stay in this cave any longer we're going to die.

They started back. The rats followed. Twice Pearl turned and drove them back like a wave sucked down a beach, but their claws scraped, their eyes advanced, their hungry chittering grew.

Pearl, we're there. See, there's a star.

They flung the torches at the rats and burst from the cave, breathing clean air at last. They jumped down the rocks and plunged into the sea, sank themselves, washed themselves, as the cave air bubbled out of their clothes. Then Hari untied the boat. They raised the sail and headed out to sea, as far away as they could get from the grey hill.

All I want to do is go to sleep, Hari said.

Me too.

After a while they pulled the sail down and let the boat
drift. They lay wet and shivering, curled together for warmth,
but slept all the same until dawn.

It took them most of the day to sail around the seaward hill
and catch sight of Saltport again.

It looks deserted, Pearl said.

Ottmar's taken all the men to fight in his war.

No, she said, there's one. He's coming out of that office
on the wharf.

The man was a Whip. He aimed a bolt gun at them and
fired, but the range was too great and the bolt hissed into
the sea.

We'll go round that headland, then walk back.

They sailed on south, and after a while the Whip turned
and went into his office.

It still feels deserted, Pearl said. He might be the only one.

They hid the boat in mangroves up a muddy creek, then
went into the hills until they found a freshwater stream
trickling down. They drank and washed again. They still felt
the salt poison on their skins.

We're going to need more food soon, Pearl said.

Maybe we'll find some in Saltport.

They kept close to the shoreline, although the farmhouses
inland showed no sign of people. The outskirts of the town
were empty too – empty houses, empty shops, an empty
school. Nothing moved in the main street. Hari and Pearl
advanced cautiously, feeling their way, but they found no life
in Saltport until they reached the wharves. Two men sat on
a bench, sharing a bottle of wine. Although they wore Whip

uniforms, they were cadets, little more than boys.

Hari and Pearl crept away to the other side of the building and went along the wall to the wharf where the Whip had his office. The door was open and the man sat inside, holding a mutton bone in his fists and tearing lumps of meat off with his teeth. He dropped the bone when he saw Hari in the doorway.

Be still, Hari said.

The man froze halfway out of his chair.

Who are you? Hari said.

'Corporal Tuck,' said the man.

Who's in charge here?

'I am.'

Hari opened the man's mind as if lifting a lid. How many men do you have?

'Two.'

That's all?

'We had two platoons, but a ship came and took them for Ottmar's army.'

Why is the town empty?

'Everyone ran away. The men took their families and sneaked off in the night. South, they went, into the hills. They thought Ottmar would come back and take them to fight. The farmers went too. They took their sheep and cattle. There's no one here.'

Where are the salt-mine workers?

'There was no one to guard them. They ran into the mountains.'

Hari nodded. Most of the salt-mine workers were burrows-men. He hoped they would find their way back to the city.

How many men came out of Deep Salt?

'Deep Salt?' There was a stirring of something like pleasure in Corporal Tuck.

How many escaped from there?

'No one escaped. They're still inside.'

You left the door closed?

'That was the order. Don't open the door.'

So you're still sending food and water in?

Corporal Tuck blinked, his eyes heavy, half alive. 'No water. No food.'

You let them die?

'My orders,' Corporal Tuck said. 'They were only slaves. There are plenty more in the burrows.'

Hari, Pearl said, moving to his side.

Kill him, said a voice in Hari. It was his own.

No, he said. He picked it out of his head like a maggot and crushed it under his foot.

How long since the last food went in?

The corporal shook his head. 'Long time. The day the men in lead suits came and took salt away.'

That long, Hari thought. So they're dead.

'I sent Fat and Candy to have a look. They said they heard voices calling out behind the door. When they went back – it was three or four days – there was nothing. They banged on the door, said they'd brought some roast beef and a keg of beer. Having a bit of fun. But no one answered. It's no matter. They were slaves. And Ottmar's clerk took away the keys anyway.'

Pearl put her hand on Hari's arm.

I'm not going to hurt him, he said. But I don't want to talk to him. You do the rest.

He set the man free. At once Tuck's hand went to his bolt gun.

Be still, Tuck, Pearl said.

Ask him why he's still here. There's no need for guards in an empty town, Hari said.

Pearl asked.

'To look after the cannon,' Tuck said. 'It was too big for the hold, so they left it. They'll send a bigger ship when Ottmar needs it.'

Hari stepped forward: 'Show me.'

They led Tuck out to the wharf.

First throw away your gun, Pearl said.

Tuck took it from its holster.

Into the sea, Pearl said.

He threw it, although he made a grieving sound.

Now show us the cannon.

It was in a shed – a bolt cannon, sitting on a flat-bed truck, with its batteries in a black case as tall as a man behind it.

'Can you fire it?' Hari said, still aloud. He did not want to go into the man's mind.

'Yes,' Tuck said.

'Then call your men.'

'Fat, Candy, get your butts round here,' Tuck bellowed.

Feet drummed on the boardwalk outside the building. The cadets skidded around the corner and stopped, looking at Tuck. Their hands, hesitating, went to their guns.

Give them to me, Pearl said, using only half her strength.

She took the guns to the edge of the wharf and dropped them into the water. Then, coming back, she took a sideways peep at Hari and read what he meant to do. She left him instructing Tuck and went searching for food, and found a store of cheese and hard-bread in the office cupboard. She took some to Hari and made him eat while the three men fired up a steam engine and ran it to the shed, where they coupled it to the flat-bed truck.

They pulled away from Saltport in mid-afternoon, following the rail track leading to the mine. The spur track was half an hour away. The cadet called Candy changed the points, and the engine pulled the cannon towards the iron door. They stopped several hundred metres away, with the cliffs of the grey hill rising like a wall.

Hari, don't break the door, Pearl said.

No. It's their grave.

He felt it was Tarl's grave as well – the Tarl who had carried him on his shoulders and taught him to survive in the burrows. He looked at the grey cliffs, searching for a weakness.

'Arm the gun, Tuck. How many bolts will it fire?'

'Twenty good ones,' Tuck said. 'Then weaker ones until we get the battery recharged.'

'Shoot at the cliff, where the crack runs underneath the overhang.'

Tuck set Fat and Candy turning wheels. He sat behind the cannon as the muzzle came up, then read the range through an instrument on the side.

'All right, fire,' Hari said.

The cannon boomed deep in the breech; light flashed from the muzzle, and a fizzing bolt, blunt-headed and as long as a snake, mounted almost lazily towards the cliff. Halfway there it began to fall, bulging in the middle as though it had been fed. It struck below the overhang in a burst of light. Rocks the size of wool bales flew out. The cliff seemed to tremble, but the overhang held.

'Again,' Hari said.

This time the overhang fell with a roar and buried the archway leading to the door in the base of the cliff. Broken stones fanned out. They rattled and lay still.

'Again.'

He kept Tuck shooting, lower on the cliff at first, then higher, and the fan of rocks increased until it pushed the lamp post flat and crushed the sentry box. The iron door was buried under tons of rock no one would ever shift.

The cadets stood waiting for orders. Tuck stood up, his face red from the cannon's heat. He saluted.

Hari felt like telling them to start walking, wherever they liked, and never come back. Instead he said: Pearl, help me. I want to make them so they'll never talk about Deep Salt.

They worked together, deep in the three men's minds, turning aside from ugly things there, telling them there was no Deep Salt, there never had been – no iron door, no men dying in the dark. And they had never seen Hari and Pearl.

When we're gone, Hari said, these are your orders, Tuck. You'll take the cannon back to the wharf and roll it into the sea. Sink it. Then you'll come back here, all three of you, and start your work. You'll tear up the spur line leading to the hill. Take away the rails, take away the sleepers. You'll make it look as if no line was ever here. It doesn't matter how long it takes, that's what you'll do. Then you'll go, and not remember, and you can walk forever if you like, but you'll never come back to Saltport.

Tuck, Candy, Fat stood like statues.

Wait until you can't see us any more.

He went to the flat-bed and shouldered the sack Pearl had filled with food. They turned their backs on the men, on the huge rock-fan, on the grey hill, and walked away. They went along the spur line, crossed the main line, and walked on cart tracks past deserted farms and empty fields. It was midnight when they reached the mangrove creek.

We'll sleep here, Hari, Pearl said.

Yes, let's sleep.

And tomorrow we can start for Stone Creek.

Hari shook his head. No, Pearl, he said.

She looked at him, alarmed.

There's one more thing I've got to do, he said.

200

FOURTEEN

Again they sailed south. To Pearl it was as if they were falling into a pit. The coastal hills were bearded with bush, the western sky leaden. She felt a pressure from each side, squeezing the boat into a hole. She had wanted never to see the city again, with its dead port and ruined burrows and the cliffs where her family had died. She had wanted never to be anywhere close to Ottmar, who was connected in her mind with the deformed rats of Deep Salt; and, she admitted, wanted never to see Tarl. There was something in him hurt beyond cure, and a twisting that would grow even tighter and never unwind. Yet she knew why Hari had to see him one more time.

Clouds grew on the horizon like heads looking over a wall. For three days they filled with darkness, then began to roll towards the coast on a steady wind. Both she and Hari were used to the summer storms that lashed the city but had never faced one at sea. Rain drove at them like steel spikes as they sailed past the cliffs, allowing them no more than glimpses of darkened trees in the parks and houses fallen to black mounds with skeletons standing in them. They saw too, like a ghost, House Ottmar standing undamaged, with the flag on its roof stretching out in the wind. It did not seem to be the Ottmar flag.

They steered for Port, with heavy swells throwing and sliding them. Neither had the skill for this sort of sailing. The breakwater on the northern side tore the tiller out of Pearl's hands as they went by. The boat scraped on rocks, then won free, gliding in still water and flapping its sail. They found a shallow ramp beyond the wharves and hauled the boat halfway out, emptied it of water, then pulled it above the high-tide mark. Port still seemed deserted, and in the storm there seemed little chance of anyone stealing the boat. They ran for the nearest building with their sack of food, found a dry room, and Hari collected scraps of wood and made a fire on a stone hearth. They warmed and dried themselves, then ate and drank.

Where are we going? Pearl said.

Into the burrows, if Tarl's there. If he's not, I don't know. Wherever I can find him. Pearl, you don't need to come.

I'm coming, she said.

They slept for an hour on the hard floor, then set out through the streets of Port. There were no people, no fires, no shouts or shrieks. The only sounds were the lashing of rain against walls and the gulping of water into drains. They went through Bawdhouse, past Keg and Keech. No people. Blood Burrow was as silent as death.

Hari climbed high into a ruin, but the rain was too thick for him to see far. Yet perhaps on the city walls there were pinpricks of light; and further off, almost invisible behind the grey shroud, pale yellow blooms that might be fires.

They saw their first people as they approached the wall – a man, woman and child walking head down into the rain. Hari made Pearl wait in a doorway. He stopped the man, held him lightly: 'Where is everyone?' he asked.

'In the city. On the cliffs. Tonight is the signing.'

'What signing?'

'Man, where've you been? Everyone knows.'

'I've been scavenging in the country. What signing?' Hari said.

'The clerks, with us. With the burrows. It's a treaty.'

'What about Ottmar?'

The man laughed, greedily delighted. His eyes glowed, and Hari let him break out of his hold.

'Ottmar's in a cage where he belongs.'

'Captured?'

'Tarl took him, with his dogs. There was a battle down in the city. The clerks beat Ottmar's army, slaughtered the lot of them, but when they tried to get up on the cliffs they found us there with Ottmar's cannons pointing in their faces and they'd had enough fighting by then, lost too many men. So they had to take their hats off and be polite to us. Hey, to us, burrows-men.'

He laughed again.

'How did Tarl capture Ottmar?'

'Just went in through a gate with his dogs when the armies were fighting. Us, Blood Burrows, going after him with our knives. We went up them paths like burrows rats, grabbed them officers and did for the lot.' He slashed with his hand, cutting a throat. 'But Tarl got Ottmar baled up with his dogs, wouldn't let us kill him. He locked him in a cage – best place for the bugger. Him and his son.'

'Kyle-Ott?'

'Kyle-Ott. We'll bring them out tonight and have some fun. That's why I come back here to fetch my boy. I want him to see. See the signing too. Tarl and Keech sitting down with them clerks and making them eat crow.'

'Keech is there?'

'He come up behind us with his lot, and Keg's lot too. And the Bawdhouse gals. He's got more men than Blood Burrow, but we've got Ottmar. We've got Tarl. You better get up there if you want to see.'

'I will,' Hari said.

The man and his wife and child went off into the rain, with the boy grizzling until the man lifted him onto his shoulders.

Pearl, Hari said, I've got to go up there. And this time you can't come.

Why not?

Because you've got white skin. You're Company. They'll kill you if they see you.

I'm not Company.

I know, Pearl. I know. But white skin and yellow hair. Pearl, it's death. You'll never get a chance to argue.

I'll keep my hood up, Pearl said.

It's not enough.

I'll tie the draw-string tight. And look . . . She scooped up mud and rubbed it on her face. I can turn brown like you. I'll do my hands and arms as well.

The rain will wash it off.

Well, soot. There's plenty of soot. I'll rub that in. Hari –

Your eyes. Blue eyes.

I'll keep them lowered. I'll look down. Company women are good at that.

He looked at her, looked into her eyes, brighter blue now that mud darkened her face.

Hari, she said, you might need me.

I care about her more than Tarl, he thought. Yet he had to see his father, tell him that the box of salt was buried in the mine where it would never be found, and Deep Salt itself

204

closed forever. And he wanted, if he could, to make Tarl happy, make him forget.

Pearl used water running from a roof to wash her face. Hari hunted for soot and found some on the underside of a sheet of tin used to shelter a cooking fire. She rubbed it on her hands and arms, then on her face, turning them closer to black than brown. Hari made her close her eyes and smeared soot on her eyelids.

Keep them closed. I'll guide you. We'll pretend you're blind.

I'll try.

The rain eased as they climbed to the city wall. It stopped altogether as they went through the gate, but the wind blew fiercely, whipping their cloaks about their legs, even though Mansion Hill stood between them and the sea. They climbed the path Pearl and Tealeaf had escaped down.

People, Pearl said.

From the burrows, Hari said.

They stood thick in the wide street of burned mansions: men, women, children, old and young, crippled and sick, all had come – and from every burrow: Blood and Keg and Keech and Basin and Bawdhouse. The burrows smell of bodies, unwashed clothes, of bad food and starvation and disease, brought tears to Hari's eyes, but gave him too a flash of elation: We've won. Then he remembered the killing, the man miming the cutting of throats, and how a treaty must be made with the clerks, and knew there were no winners, nobody won. But surely, he thought, things will be better. The burrows needn't starve any more.

He pushed his way through, shielding Pearl, and when men objected said, 'I'm Tarl's son, Hari. I've got a message for Tarl.'

They let him pass. Guards posted casually at the Ottmar mansion knew him and hailed him and pushed him through the gate.

The people on the lawns were mostly fighting men, from every burrow, with here and there a tight-knit squad of knife-women from Bawdhouse. Some had pulled charred planks from the fallen mansions and were coaxing fires alight in the wet wood and cooking food the clerks had sent up as a gesture of goodwill. Others lounged on sofas and chairs dragged from Ottmar's mansion, not caring that they were sodden with rain. Beyond the crowd, by the cliff, the wall had been torn down between Ottmar's park and the rock where Cowl the Liberator had thrown the Families to their deaths – and where, a hundred years later, Ottmar had also thrown his victims. The marble hand still stood, although its fingers had been blasted off by a hit from a bolt cannon. Only the thumb remained, pointing crookedly out to sea. An awning raised on poles at the back of the hand sheltered a table and four chairs. Groups of men stood about, Blood Burrows men, Keech men, with Bawdhouse women further away, keeping to themselves.

Off to one side men shouted and danced about an iron cage, throwing gnawed bones and handfuls of mud through the bars.

It's Ottmar and Kyle-Ott, Pearl said.

Ottmar lay curled up in the centre of the cage, half clad in torn finery. He shivered and moaned, then gabbled something to himself – some litany of his former glory – and opened his eyes and looked about, and closed them again to force reality away. Kyle-Ott stood, gripping the bars. He looked about defiantly; he shouted too, cries of rage and contempt – but shivered like his father. His terror and disbelief were the same.

Pearl and Hari turned away. Ottmar had treated his enemies more cruelly than this, yet seeing him suffer turned him into a victim too, someone they should try to help. It bewildered them.

I don't want to see what happens to them, Pearl whispered.

No. I'll find Tarl. Then we'll go.

They went around to the front of the awning. Keech was there – a short man, with his legs bowed almost in a circle, and a blind eye, whiter than milk, and one side of his face slipping into his neck from a childhood illness. His good eye was like a click-beetle, jumping about, finding everything.

Tarl stood with a smaller group, enclosed by them but seeming alone. Beyond him, in the growing dark, Dog and his pack lay on the grass, gnawing bones.

'More light. We need fire. Bring some wood,' Keech shouted.

Men ran up with charred doors and splintered planks and piled them in front of the awning, where others with burning brands coaxed them alight. One fire, two, then half a dozen burned between the awning and the marble hand.

Hari and Pearl retreated. He wanted to talk to Tarl unseen. They circled behind the awning again, passing the cage where a man forced Kyle-Ott back from the bars with a stream of urine, and approached the dog pack out of the dark.

Wait here, Pearl.

Hari stepped towards the pack cautiously.

Dog, he said.

Dog jerked as though someone had kicked him, then stood growling.

Dog, come here.

The animal saw him and his hackles rose, but Hari said: Easy, Dog, I'm your friend. Come here.

Dog approached carefully, and stopped a metre away, ignoring Hari's proferred hand.

All right, Dog. I know you're the leader. But I need to talk to Tarl. Go and get him.

Dog growled.

I'm his son, Dog. He wants to see me.

Dog seemed to think a moment. Then his half-risen hackles flattened. He turned and trotted away. The men about Tarl parted and let him through. Hari smiled at their deference. Dogs and burrows-men had once been food for each other.

Dog nudged Tarl's hand with his nose and turned to face Hari, who could not read the message that passed between them but felt Tarl's leap of joy. His father broke out of the group and ran towards him.

'Hari.'

'Tarl.'

They hugged each other.

'Hari, where've you been? I thought you'd got yourself killed. I've been telling them you'd come back and bring a new weapon. Did you get it, Hari?'

'No, Tarl. Now listen. There's no weapon. No weapon you or anyone else can ever use. The salt is poisonous. It kills everyone. And everything. Animals, plants. It'll kill the world if it gets loose. You can't use it.'

'Hari . . .'

'Listen. I stole Ottmar's salt and took it back to Deep Salt. We stole it, Pearl and me. We took it to the mine and left it there. Then we closed the mine. No one will ever find it again.'

'But, Hari, I've got to have it. I've told them there's a weapon coming. The clerks will be too strong for us. I've told Keech . . .'

Hari closed his eyes. He had never felt so close to his father, or so far away.

Tarl, he said. He went deep into Tarl's mind, invading his father, hating what he had to do. Tarl had meant more to him than anyone, until Pearl.

Tarl, there's no Deep Salt. You were never there. Say it, Tarl.

Tarl shook himself, as if he felt the poisonous light pricking his skin again.

'There's no Deep Salt. I was never there,' he whispered.

That's all, Tarl. I'm going now. Remember I'm your son. Remember I love you.

He withdrew from Tarl's mind as if backing out of a room full of shadowy objects that had been familiar. Dog, standing beside Tarl, whimpered with puzzlement.

A cry came from behind them: 'Tarl, is this the boy you promised us? The boy with the weapon?'

Keech walked towards them, comical on his bandy legs, but fierce, demanding in his face.

'My son,' Tarl whispered, nodding at Keech but not seeming to know where he was. He held Hari tightly by the arm.

'Hari, is that your name? Tarl said you'd gone to find Ottmar's secret weapon.' He laughed. 'That's something I'll believe in when I see it. Burrows men only need knives.'

'Keech,' Hari said, 'I've heard of you. You followed Tarl, my father, up the hill. You would do well to follow him wherever he leads. But talk of a weapon – no, that was a tale to keep our burrows-men strong. We need no weapon, as you say, but our knives.'

Keech's good eye held Hari's face as tightly as a fist.

This man is dangerous, Hari thought.

'So,' Keech said, and turned to Tarl, 'no weapon, eh? Well, I know shit when I hear it. I knew it was shit. But the men – the men who follow me – are not going to like it. Keech men don't like Blood men using them like fools.'

Hari tried, gently at first, to go into Keech's mind, but found a barrier there and, when he pushed harder, felt

209

it thicken, settle in place, and felt, behind it, a force that seemed to reach for knowledge of what invaded it, the way horses reached sometimes, the way Dog reached.

He withdrew. He was afraid. Keech was beginning in the way he had begun, with no more than blindness and a power, and Hari wondered how long it would be before the man heard the distant whisper: Keech. What would he become then? And where would that strength come from, what mysterious power?

I've got to take Tarl with me, he thought. He can't fight this man.

Before he could decide what to do, a cry rose from the lawns behind the mansion: 'The clerks are coming!'

The crowds in the streets had pushed through the open gates and formed a mass that surged and rumbled, filling Ottmar's park from the mansion to the awning by the marble hand. A party of Blood Burrows men escorted three clerks through, breaking a way with blows from wooden staves. They brought them to the awning, three nervous men trying to look unconcerned. Keech hurried towards them, pulling on a feathered hat that made him look like a street juggler.

'Hari,' Tarl said, 'wait here. I need you.' He hurried after Keech, with Dog close by his side.

Hari found Pearl gripping his arm. The crowd had pushed her forward. Then he felt another pressure on them both, moving them closer to the awning: Keech men, a dozen or more, had circled behind them. They made a wall that stopped Hari and Pearl from finding a way back through the crowd. Hari was bewildered. When had Keech given that order?

Pearl, they're holding us. But it's me they want, not you.

I'm staying.

There are too many for us to control.

Hari, just wait for our chance. We'll get away.

210

Tarl had joined Keech under the awning. But it was Keech who was in command. His shaggy beard, growing on only one side of his face, stood out almost straight in the fierce wind blowing from the sea. His feathered hat was whipped into the crowd. He let it go. One of his bent legs kicked away the chairs on the burrows side of the table.

'Burrows-men stay on their feet. We like to move fast. But sit, you clerks, if you want to rest your arses.'

The crowd roared its approval.

Two of the clerks, in red and blue uniforms with tassels at the belt, sat down. The third man, standing behind their chairs, was the clerk Tarl had thrown his knife at, who had had his elbow crushed in People's Square. Hari saw him recognise Tarl from the acid mark on his forehead – and, probing at the three men, saw that he was the clever one. He carried his arm in a sling, and when one of the officers put his hand back for a document he drew it out of the sling with a flourish.

The clerks wanted ceremony and speeches, but Keech was having none of it. He grabbed the document from the clerk and tore it in two.

'Burrows-men don't read,' he cried. 'This is paper. We burn paper to keep warm.' He tossed the pieces behind him, and one of his men grabbed them and ran to the nearest fire and threw them on.

'All we need is to say what we're going to do . . .'

Hari, Pearl said, Keech and the other one, the clerk at the back, they're the ones in charge. Can you feel them? Each one will betray the treaty. They'll bargain and lie, then one will kill the other and Keech or the clerk will rule. I can feel it in them, going round and round.

Tarl has no chance, Hari said.

'This is the agreement,' Keech roared, speaking more to

211

the burrows crowd than to the clerks. 'Keech – Keech and Tarl, Keech and Blood Burrow, and Bawdhouse, and all the burrows – we keep the heights. They are ours. We keep the burrows. They are ours. We keep the southern side of Port. That is ours. And we keep the southern half of City, from the great avenue that runs into the west. It is ours when we take it from the workers, who are scum. All the rest the clerks can have. That is yours.'

'But,' cried one of the officers, 'that's absurd. That wasn't the agreement . . .'

'The agreement is changed. Remember that our cannons look down on your homes and families. On your children, eh, so soft and white. They look down like fangcats ready to pounce. How much have you lost already? Do you want to lose more? We will fight with you against the workers. Kill them. Drive them out. And we will divide things as I have said. Agree now or go back where you came from, but listen for our cannons as you go down.'

The clerk with the crushed arm leaned between the officers and whispered. White-faced, they shook their heads. The clerk whispered again.

Keech will kill them if they don't agree, Hari said.

They know, Pearl said.

The senior officer stood up. He swayed and looked as if he would faint. But the clerk murmured again – and Pearl and Hari heard: Tell them we agree. Everything can be changed when it suits us. We have time.

The officer raised his hand. His voice came faintly: 'We agree to the terms.'

'Louder,' Keech bellowed. 'I want my people to hear.'

'We agree to the terms,' the officer cried weakly.

'You hear, burrows-men,' Keech yelled. 'You hear, Keech Burrow. The treaty is agreed. We have the burrows, and the

212

heights, and the city and the port. They are ours. The burrows are free from tyranny at last.'

A roar rose from the crowd, like water rushing uphill; and the rain started again, slanting in like sharpened wire and hissing in the fires.

Keech raised his arms. He was like a magician, making silence.

'Now we must entertain our friends, the clerks, and show them how Keech Burrow punishes its enemies. Bring the prisoners.'

Men pulled open the cage door at the back of the awning. They dragged out Kyle-Ott, who bit and fought, and Ottmar, half lifting him like a sack. They pushed them across the table, knocking the clerks aside, and Keech grabbed each by the collar, one handed, hauled them the rest of the way and threw them on the grass in front of the crowd. The wind blew a great gust, puffing then hollowing the canvas roof, which clapped twice like a giant hand.

'The great King Ottmar. The Prince Kyle-Ott. See how they kneel before you, burrows-men.'

Hari and Pearl had worked their way forward, trying to get away from the men hedging them. They stood close to Tarl and Dog, at the awning's side.

'Tarl, he's taken control. We've got to get out of here.'

'No. No.'

'Tarl, he'll kill you next.'

'No he won't. I've got Blood Burrow. I've got the dogs. Hari, stand by me, help me, Hari. I can beat him.'

Keech men hauled Ottmar and Kyle-Ott to their feet. Ottmar was gibbering with terror.

Tarl stepped forward.

'My prisoners. Mine,' he cried. 'I put them in their cages and I will order their deaths.'

'Slaves,' Kyle-Ott cried shrilly. 'You are slaves, you are filth.'

'What does it matter,' Keech bellowed, 'who captured them? Here they are, the last of the Families alive, and when they're dead there are no more left. So let us kill them, burrows. Let's throw them from the Rock.'

Kyle-Ott climbed to his feet. He kept his courage.

'My father could not have ruled,' he cried. 'Look at him. He weeps like a girl. But I can rule. Take me for your king. I will give you riches, burrows-men. You shall have seats beside my throne. I'll appoint you as my governors and generals, you –' pointing at Keech – 'and you –' at Tarl. 'My right hand and my left, in war, in trade, in plunder, in all the riches that belonged to Company. And I will take one of your women as my queen. Bring them forth. Bring forth your maidens. Let me choose.'

His eyes swept them – Keech, Tarl, the men standing at their backs, searching for women – then they stopped. Stopped at Pearl. She could not get her eyes closed quickly enough. Kyle-Ott knew her. His face turned white; the scar on his cheek stood out red.

He gave a shriek: 'It is her. It is Pearl. It is Radiant Pearl, my father's bride. Burrows-men, I am not the last. There is one more. I give her to you. She's my gift. Throw her in my place, throw the bride with the king –' he gestured at his father – 'and I will be your new king . . .'

'Kill the boy,' Keech cried. 'Stop his babble. Take him.'

Men rushed forward, seized Kyle-Ott by the arms, ran him through a channel opening in the crowd, past the marble hand to the edge of the cliff, and threw him, screaming defiance, into the dark.

'That's the end of the boy king. Now for his daddy,' cried Keech.

But Ottmar had not waited. The men who held him had

loosened their grip to watch Kyle-Ott die, and Ottmar, mad with terror, knocked them aside. He ran, fast for a big man, across the face of the crowd, and as his son fell he broke clear, heading for the wall between the park and the House Kruger gardens.

Keech laughed. He let Ottmar get among the trees by the wall, then cried: 'Bring him back, Keech men. Bring back our king and make him fly.'

A dozen men ran after Ottmar. But Tarl was quicker.

'Dog,' he said, touching him lightly on the head.

Dog gave a shrill bark, alerting his pack. He ran, overtaking the men, joining then leading the pack, which made a hideous yelping of excitement. Ottmar reached the wall and heaved himself up, once, twice, straining his arms. The dogs took him on his third try – ankle, calf and thigh – while Dog, leaping, fastened his teeth in Ottmar's side and hung like a gourd twisting on a vine. Ottmar fell. The dogs boiled over him in a heaving mass of brown and black and yellow.

Pearl and Hari had turned away. They tried to break through the men surrounding them, but there was no way, even when they tried to push them with their minds. When one was dazed and under control, another stepped into his place.

'The end of Ottmar, burrows-men,' Tarl cried. 'Blood Burrow takes Ottmar. He is food for my dogs.'

Keech grinned at him. His teeth flashed in the firelight, halving his crooked mouth. 'It is well done,' he said. 'Tarl does well. But listen, burrows-men, there is another. Ottmar is dead. Ottmar is bones. But what about this queen the boy prince told us of? Where is she? Where is Queen Pearl?'

He turned suddenly. His black jumping eye settled on Pearl. He motioned with his hand, and the men at her back lifted her and threw her down beside the overturned chairs.

'Stand her up,' Keech said.

They pulled her to her feet. Keech stepped forward and jerked the hood from her face. Pearl's yellow hair tumbled out. He tore her cloak open and stripped it away, leaving her in her trousers and shirt.

'See, the boy Kyle-Ott was right. She comes from the Families, she is Pearl. See her hair, burrows-men, see it shine like Company gold. See her arms, they are white. See her ears, like sea shells, and her eyes like the sea. Keech Burrow claims her. Keech will make her fly.'

Pearl could do nothing. Her mind was paralysed and would not work. She felt herself contracting; she was small and pinched with terror.

Then she heard Hari's voice, far away: Do nothing, Pearl. Trust me, Pearl.

He spoke aloud: 'Leave her, Keech. She's my prisoner.'

'Who, the boy, Hari? The boy without a weapon. You have no voice here.'

'My own voice,' Hari cried, 'and the voice of Tarl, my father. And the voice of Blood Burrow too. And she is mine. Pearl is mine. I took her. I brought her here as my prisoner. She is my offering to the burrows. Radiant Pearl of House Bowles.'

His mind had never worked so fast, yet every step he must take was certain, as though he walked easily across a room.

'The boy talks shit. Don't listen to the boy. He brought her here hidden, to spy on us,' Keech cried.

Hari went into the man's mind, making him reel, holding him, although he met the same wall as before. He knew his advantage would not last.

Quiet, Keech.

He raised his voice: 'I brought her as the last survivor of the Families. I brought her to die. And I will be her executioner. I

216

will throw her. It is my right, for Blood Burrow. Ask Tarl.'

Tarl saw his chance.

'Hari speaks the truth. Stand by him, Blood Burrow. Burrows all. He captured her: the right of execution lies with him.'

'Enough talk,' cried a Bawdhouse woman. 'Let the boy do it. Throw the girl.'

Other voices rose, became a roar of approval.

Hari stepped to Pearl's side. He gripped her arm.

Do what I say, Pearl. Do nothing else.

He raised his voice: 'Clear the way. Let me take her to the Rock.'

Stumble, Pearl. Make it look as if you're afraid.

I am afraid, Hari.

So am I.

He pushed by Keech, who was free again, although shaking his head as though a botfly buzzed in it. A path opened past the fires, towards the marble hand. Hari led Pearl along it, holding her up, not talking to her. He played the steps of what he must do in his mind, held them in sequence, made them perfect. Then he spoke to Pearl.

Pearl, when I came here looking in windows, I worked out ways to get away if anyone saw me. There's only one we can use now.

What, Hari?

We jump off the cliff.

Hari . . .

Not from the Rock. From where the thumb points, from the hand. It's close to the edge, it's only four or five steps. When you stand there you can see two reefs sticking out, with water in between up to the cliff. Pearl, the tide has to be high, and it is. The wind has to be blowing in, and it is. Each wave rolls up to the cliff, and there's a moment when

217

it hits, it bulges up and then it's still, half a second, before it rushes out. Pearl . . .

Hari, we can't . . .

Yes we can. I timed it. I threw down stones to see how long they took. There's no other way. Hold on to me, Pearl.

There was a space between the front of the crowd and the hand. They moved across it slowly, Pearl stumbling. Keech followed them. Tarl came at his side. Glancing back, Hari saw Tarl move his hand onto his Dweller knife.

'Hurry, boy,' Keech said. 'We haven't got all night.'

Hari ignored him.

Pearl, fall over when we go under the thumb. Make it seem you're crying.

I am crying, Hari.

They moved further ahead of Keech and Tarl. The grass gave way to rock, where the plinth that held the hand had its base. The crowd belched with anticipation as they passed under the marble thumb. Pearl sank to the ground.

Good, Pearl.

I can't help it.

He put his foot on her, rolled her over, grinned at the crowd, which shouted with glee. The place Kyle-Ott had been thrown from was ten metres ahead, but the edge of the cliff, where they would jump, was only five steps away. He pulled Pearl to her feet, then looked at the sea, where two black points of reef should be visible. The rain was too thick – he could not see them; but glimpsed a grey puff, like a dust ball, two puffs, as a wave struck where the reefs must end.

The next one, he thought.

Stagger, Pearl. Push me closer to the edge.

He heard the wave he had seen strike the base of the cliff.

Pearl, when I say go, just walk to the edge and we'll jump.

218

Go out as far as you can. And hold my hand. Don't let go.

He saw two more grey puffs and counted to six, remembering the falling stones.

Go, Pearl. Three steps and jump.

He heard the crowd hiss like a curled snake, and, rising above it, Tarl's agonised cry: 'Hari!' The sounds were lost in the wind smacking against the cliff. They fell, holding hands, and caught the still moment of the wave. It sucked them down, tore them apart, bounced them deep on a shingle floor between rock walls, sucked at them, tumbled them, squeezed them empty of air, and threw them up like grains of barley in a boiling pot, out beyond the ends of the reef.

Hari found Pearl and held her afloat. He fought the sea, trying to stay alive. Pearl thought: We'll die now. This is the end.

Not yet. I'm taking off my cloak. I think I can swim.

Later, Hari could not remember how they survived. It took them all that night and half the next day. He found a pallet, almost waterlogged, tossing under the cliff, and rolled Pearl onto it, and somehow kicked and paddled it away from the rocks. The wind subsided but the rain kept on. Pearl lay curled up, shivering. He never gave up hope of saving her. By midday they were off the breakwater. The pallet grew heavier and sank deeper. It took another hour to work it into the harbour opening, and another to bring it to the ramp where the boat lay. Hari lifted Pearl and carried her to the room they had used, not caring if he was seen, caring now only to get her somewhere warm and dry.

Their two blankets lay folded in the corner where they had left them. Hari stripped off Pearl's clothing and used the thinner one to rub her dry. Her body was mottled with bruises from the shingle. He wrapped her in the other blanket, then built a fire and laid her in front of it. There was food. He mashed hard-bread and cheese with water and fed her the paste. She ate a little, then slept. He slept beside her.

They stayed three days in the room. On the second night Hari took his fishing knife and killed a rat. He found a rusty cooking pot in a ruined building and sat it in embers and made a stew, with bitter-weed picked in a warehouse yard. Pearl grew stronger. On the third night she helped him with two scavengers – controlled them, sent them on their way with no memory of where they had been. On that night, too, they heard cannons booming on Mansion Heights and other cannons answering from the city. In the misty rain the sky turned red.

It was fine in the morning. They sailed through the breakwater and turned north with a breeze driving them along.

The guns were silent. The only sound they heard was the howling of dogs, far away and mournful in the burrows.

FIFTEEN

It was Hari's turn to be sick. He sat at the tiller and could not keep his head up. Fevers made him shiver, then sweat. They went slowly, resting half the day on beaches, sleeping on creek banks in the night. The wind died away. They lay scarcely moving on a dead sea, burning in the mid-summer heat.

Now Pearl was frightened Hari would die, but he ground his teeth and tried to smile at her.

It's all right, Pearl. It's Ottmar in me. It's Keech in me. I'm getting them out. He groaned and sweated.

The three hills came into view, with Saltport hunched at the waterline. The grey hill had a wide scar, shining like glass. They crept past.

Hari fought the sickness out of himself. By the time the hills were lost in the southern coastline he felt his strength coming back. They dug for shellfish in an estuary and picked ripe fruit from trees further up the creek. Slowly they made their way towards Stone Creek. Each night they pulled the boat up on a beach, and made a fire and sat side by side, talking silently, then talking aloud. They found they liked the sound of voices, and laughter was happier coming from the mouth.

They slept side by side wrapped in blankets, and woke cold one morning, halfway between midnight and dawn, and saw each other's eyes glint in the starlight. They began touching each other, and soon found the way to make love.

They stayed on the beach all that day and another night, then started for Stone Creek again. Two days they sailed on a calm sea, and found Tealeaf waiting for them at the tideline. She welcomed them, speaking aloud, understanding at once their need to hear normal speech. They walked to Sartok's house, talking all the way, although Pearl and Hari kept their descriptions bare: the box of salt, Ottmar's bullets, the journey to Deep Salt, the rats – all of it. They told her about their jump from the cliff and their voyage home, and Tealeaf saw from their faces what had happened on the way.

She told them Dwellers hidden in the city had sent reports of the fighting there. The clerks and the burrows-men attacked the workers' army, but the workers had a battery of cannons too. No one won the battle. Then the clerks betrayed the treaty and joined the workers and drove the burrows-men from the Heights. Many got away and hid in the burrows again. No one knew what had happened to Keech.

'But now everything breaks up,' Tealeaf said. 'There are bands of men and women hunting for food, and there's none in the city any more. The warehouses are empty. People are leaving. Robber bands are raiding in the country, burning towns and villages. Everything is crumbling. There'll be starvation and massacre, and this will go on for many years.'

'Where's Tarl?' Hari asked.

'Tarl fled with his dogs. He went across the plains into the forest, and deeper, some say, into the jungle. Already Tarl becomes a legend. Men call him the Dog King.'

They fell silent after that. Hari grieved for his father, and that night and all the next day Pearl stayed at his side. Then they took the boat and sailed north. They camped on a beach for three days, and when they came back Hari had put Tarl safely away, where he could visit with calmer memories, although now and then tears came into his eyes.

They worked in the gardens. They worked in the smokehouse drying fish, and Eentel taught Pearl how to play tunes on a bamboo flute. Then Tealeaf came to them and asked what they wanted to do.

'Hari and I have talked,' Pearl said. 'We love it here but we want to go inland and find a place and make a farm and stay for the rest of our lives. We want to be as far from the city as we can get. And Tealeaf, we don't want to go inside people's minds and steal their memories. Not if we don't have to.'

Tealeaf smiled. 'I thought that was it. And I know a place on the other side of the Inland Sea. Dwellers go there but we haven't settled. A river flows out. The land is fertile. We'll help you, Pearl. We'll help you, Hari. The people with no name will guide you through the jungle. Dwellers will take you across the Inland Sea –' she smiled again – 'and teach you how to build a house and plant crops. And one day, not long perhaps, we'll send others to you.'

'Who?'

'Pearl, it's a seed time. Remember Tilly? Her baby's born. We're keeping them safe. We think he'll be able to speak like Hari and you. And there'll be others. I'm going back to the city . . .'

'No, Tealeaf.'

'Yes. I know ways to hide myself. We'll bring them to you. Tilly and her baby, and others when we find them. Children who can speak and maybe hear the voice . . .'

'There's another voice,' Hari said.

'Yes, Hari. Ottmar heard it. The man you call Keech heard it too. And you, Hari, you heard it, and you fought and pushed it away. But it hides itself and waits. Where there's one voice, there will always be the other in men. In Dwellers too. Hari, you might hear it again, but you've made your choice.' She touched him lightly on the wrist. 'And if you never hear your name spoken again in the voice you long to hear, it's there in you, it won't go away. Do you feel it, in your pulse?'

Hari smiled. 'Yes, I do.'

'And you, Pearl, what do you feel, now you are with child?'

'How did you know that? I'm not sure I know.'

'I'm Tealeaf, I'm your personal maid.'

'And look what you've done to Hari. I wanted to tell him.'

'I'd better go away then, and let you do it,' Tealeaf said.

They left Stone Creek two weeks later. Tealeaf took them part of the way, then turned south for the city. Pearl and Hari went on, through the forest, through the jungle, over the Inland Sea, and built their home and planted crops, and Pearl had her daughter.

They waited for the others who would come to them.

THE SECOND INSTALMENT OF MAURICE GEE'S
BREATHTAKING *SALT* SERIES

Sixteen years have passed since Pearl from Company and Hari
from Blood Burrow defeated the tyrant Ottmar. Now their
children, Xantee and Lo, face an even more dangerous foe.

Hari lies gravely ill with a fragment of a strange creature
wrapped around his throat, draining his life. The beast is called
gool, meaning unbelonger. It is one of many, destroying the
mountains and jungles of the world. Somewhere a hidden
mother nourishes her gool brood – she must be found and
destroyed to save Hari and the world they know.

Xantee, Lo and the brave and practical youth Duro, all of
them 'speakers', set out on a perilous mission that will take
them through jungles and over mountains to the ruined city
of Belong, and on to Ceebeedee, where terrifying clashes with
the cruel rival leaders and lurking gool await them.

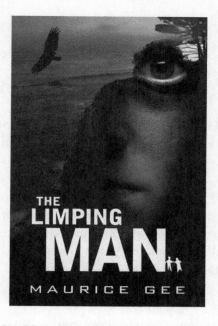

THE THIRD INSTALMENT OF MAURICE GEE'S
BREAKTAKING *SALT* SERIES

What is the source of the Limping Man's monstrous power? Nobody can withstand it, a soft crawling that seeps into your skin and wriggles into your mind, making you powerless with love for him even as his cruelties multiply.

When Hana's mam chooses to swallow frogweed poison rather than die in the great witch-burning in People's Square, Hana flees the burrows before she too is taken. Deep in the forest she meets Ben, son of Lo, and the two journey back to the burrows to find a way to destroy the Limping Man before his evil consumes the world.

But first they must discover the secret of his strength.

PRAISE FOR *SALT*

'A compelling tale of anger and moral development that also powerfully explores the evils of colonialism and racism.'

Publishers Weekly

'In spare yet vivid prose, Gee creates a world of oppressive caste systems and endless violence in which our heroes work to save people from their own dark nature. This is a suspenseful, somber fantasy that combines exciting action with a subtle spiritual element.'

Booklist

'It is a marvellous moment when you read the first page of a new book and realise that you are holding a classic of the future.'

Weekend Press

'A superb crossover fantasy, a skilfully told story, taut and fast-moving. It uses sympathetic and intriguing characters to creat a powerful parable, which some may choose to interpret as a logical extension of the dehumanising effect of the market economy. It also works brilliantly as a hard-edged novel of action. Above all it is Maurice Gee's fantasy masterpiece.'

Magpies

'*Salt* is a sophisticated fantasy that delivers the goods.'

Otago Daily Times